SHOOT

Cover design by David Stockman

Also by Brian Nicholson featuring

John Gunn

GWEILO

AL SAMAK

ASHANTI GOLD

FIRE DRAGON

CALYPSO

SHARK

TRAITOR

ASSASSIN

SHOOT

SHOOT

BRIAN NICHOLSON

Order this book online at www.trafford.com
or email orders@trafford.com

Most Trafford titles are also available at major online book retailers.

© Copyright 2014 Brian Nicholson.
Cover design by David Stockman
All rights reserved. No part of this publication may be reproduced, stored in a
retrieval system, or transmitted, in any form or by any means, electronic, mechanical,
photocopying, recording, or otherwise, without the written prior permission of the author.

This book is a work of fiction and all the characters, places and events in this book are
fictitious, and any resemblance to actual persons, living or dead, is purely coincidental.

Printed in the United States of America.

ISBN: 978-1-4907-2777-6 (sc)
ISBN: 978-1-4907-2780-6 (e)

Library of Congress Control Number: 2014902851

Because of the dynamic nature of the Internet, any web addresses or links contained in
this book may have changed since publication and may no longer be valid. The views
expressed in this work are solely those of the author and do not necessarily reflect the
views of the publisher, and the publisher hereby disclaims any responsibility for them.

Any people depicted in stock imagery provided by Thinkstock are models,
and such images are being used for illustrative purposes only.
Certain stock imagery © Thinkstock.

Trafford rev. 02/10/2014

 www.trafford.com
North America & international
toll-free: 1 888 232 4444 (USA & Canada)
fax: 812 355 4082

For Guinness

FOREWORD

In 1988, after a series of leaks and defections in MI5 and MI6, the Prime Minister tasked a relatively young Major General, who had retired at the age of 48, with the reorganisation of the United Kingdom's Intelligence Services. After retirement he had redirected his talents into management consultancy and turned two failing companies from near bankruptcy to healthy, profit-making concerns.

Within a year of being given the remit to set up an effective, efficient and secure intelligence service, he had created the British Intelligence Directorate. Both the espionage and counter-espionage departments were brought under the same roof where their efforts were complimentary rather than contradictory. Very few MI5 and MI6 personnel survived the stringent security vetting initiated by the new director. The two buildings at Millbank and Vauxhall Cross were retained, but only for a limited period during the changeover, as an overt intelligence front. In reality they had little more than a clerical role for storage and retrieval of historical intelligence material.

Kingsroad House was purpose-built for BID in Cale Street to the north of the King's Road. Outwardly it claimed to be the head office of Express Delivery Services (EDS). Access to EDS was by the main entrance on Cale Street while access to BID was either via the main entrance or via the 10th floor of the adjacent multi-storey NCP car park. There were two other headquarter buildings; one in Kingston-on-Thames and another in Southampton. Both had a similar layout to Kingsroad House, but possessed subtle variations in case security was compromised.

Kingsroad House had fourteen above-ground floors, with a helipad on the fifteenth floor. There were three basement levels, which contained BID's emergency medical centre—the main medical facility was at Maidenhead—an extensive transport department, stores, a small armoury and a weapons testing area. The lowest basement level also provided access to four passages that could be used by BID staff to leave the building avoiding any form of surveillance.

BID became operational in April 1990.

PROLOGUE

'Whassat?'

'Nuffink . . . . jus'an owl or somfink. Shudup an' keep yer trap shut,' was whispered harshly by the elder of the two boys.

They crept through the bracken and undergrowth of the five acre broadleaf Hunstman Copse towards the game pen which was stocked with pheasants at the start of the shooting season. The copse had been planted in the eighteenth century by Lancelot (Capability) Brown during the landscaping of the estate and was perfectly sited on the edge of a sculpted valley which provided the waiting guns with challenging high shots as the birds were driven from the copse.

Both boys were carrying air rifles. They came from two families in the village of Lower Shalford which had once been a part of the Granvil Estate. The village now lay outside the boundary wall of the 1,200 acre estate on the western edge of the New Forest in Hampshire, but many of its inhabitants benefitted from employment on the estate and the revenue which the wealthy shooting clientele and garden centre visitors brought to the village.

The lands of the estate had been a gift to Simon du Jardin, Duc de Granville, in the eleventh century by a grateful William I for his assistance in the defeat of King Harold II at Hastings. The family name had since been anglicised to Jardine and the title to the Duke of Cranborne. William Jardine was the 16th Duke of Cranborne and at that moment was enjoying a drink with his family and his head gamekeeper, John Hammond, after a thoroughly successful day's shooting. The estate provided some of the best shooting and variety of game in the Country—pheasant, partridge and woodcock in abundance. The only game lacking was grouse because there was no heather and no moor.

Scaling the perimeter wall of the estate was part of the 'dare' of tonight's expedition by Billy Cox and Trevor Perry. Billy, aged eleven, was the elder of the two by a year and had dared Trevor to accompany him on what he claimed was one of his frequent forays into the estate to outwit the gamekeepers and their dogs. The truth was dramatically different: there had only been one previous foray which had ended with Billy being taken back to his parent's house by the head gamekeeper.

It was a mild October Saturday night and the boys' parents were both in the 'Plough' for the weekly quiz. Both boys had been left in the Cox's house with Amy, Billy's sixteen-year-old sister, who spent her entire time glued to her i-phone and who was completely unaware of what the boys were doing. Also in the pub were many of the beaters who had taken part in the Granvil Estate's first shoot of the season.

*

'Sorry to interrupt Your Grace,' it was Barry Foxton, one of three assistant gamekeepers who was on duty that night.

'Not at all Barry . . . . problems?' the Duke queried.

'Just some kids, sir.'

'John's over there. I expect he'll want to go with you. Thanks again for your hard work today.'

'Pleasure, sir,' and Barry and John Hammond, the head gamekeeper left Granvil Hall, jumped into the Landrover and drove to the estate's shooting lodge.

'What's the problem?' John asked as soon as they were both in the Landrover.

'CCTV and motion sensors have picked up two trespassers. Look like kids. They're not far from the Huntsman pen. You said you wanted to be told if there were any more trespassers on the estate.'

'I did . . . . thanks Barry. Let's see if it's the Cox boy again. Are there guns on board . . . . just in case it's not those boys but poachers?

'Yea, two loaded in the rack at the back.'

*

The two boys were now on their stomachs, squirming through the bracken towards the eight foot high wire netting of the pen. Billy nudged Trevor.

'Trev, I'll go ahead an' recce the ground,' he whispered to his younger companion. He wasn't completely sure what that meant, but it was a phrase frequently used on his video games. He crawled forward until he came to the cleared area around the pen. He switched on the little 'Magilite' torch which had been hanging round his neck—a stocking present from his father the previous Christmas. He had never been there before despite his boasts to Trevor. The powerful little torch revealed the electric wires around the base of the pen and the traps to deny access to the birds by ground vermin. The alien scene unnerved the young boy. Neither of the boys had thought to discuss what they were going to do if they shot a pheasant or how they would get the dead bird out of the pen. In the cold dark of night, his warm house and the TV seemed infinitely preferable to where he now found himself. Billy turned round, still on his stomach and crawled back to where he thought he had left Trevor. He had only gone a couple of yards into the bracken when he bumped into Trevor . . . . or what he thought was Trevor.

'I told you to wait,' he hissed under his breath at Trevor, but there was no response. He reached out to shake Trevor awake, believing that he had fallen asleep. He jerked his hand back in horror as it touched a sticky pulp. He shone the torch at his hand. It was covered in blood and bone chips. Billy jumped to his feet and shone his torch at the ground. In front of him was a body lying in the bracken. The head of the body was a bloody pulp of bone chips and brain matter. He let out an involuntary shriek of terror, dropped his air rifle, abandoned the petrified Trevor still lying in the bracken and ran from the gruesome corpse; straight into the arms of the gamekeeper.

CHAPTER 1

'My gamekeeper told me that the man was decapitated.'

'That's right, Your Grace; a 12 gauge cartridge at point blank range is pretty destructive,' Detective Chief Inspector Nesbit of Felbridge CID agreed.

'But you have been able to identify him?' the Duke asked.

'Yes, Your Grace . . . .'

'Sorry to interrupt, Chief Inspector, but do please forego all the courtesy title business. We all do in this household. I'm William Jardine, my wife is Celine, our elder son is Richard—he manages everything to do with the shoot. Our younger son is Andrew and he runs the farm. Our daughter is Cecile and she manages the garden centre. I hope that helps to put you in the picture.'

'Thank you sir, it does. We identified the man from items in his wallet. He's a Mr Nigel Lucas. He . . . .'

'Another interruption . . . . sorry Chief Inspector . . . . let me get my son Richard to join us as he was with the shooting clientele all day,' and the Duke beckoned to his elder son who was in the family group with the gamekeepers at the other end of the drawing room. When he joined his father and the policeman, the Duke repeated the name to his son. 'Nigel Lucas, Richard; are you familiar with that name?'

Before replying, Richard Jardine produced a folded guest list from his pocket.

'Because of the VIP status of the diplomatic guests, the FCO asked if they might add a 'minder' to the shooting party. We of course agreed. Nigel Lucas was that minder and I believe that he comes from the Diplomatic Protection Section of the Counter Espionage Department of the Intelligence Directorate. This is a copy of all the people involved in the shooting today, including me, and all the staff of the estate and those people hired in to beat,' and he handed two sheets of foolscap to the Chief Inspector.

*

'Yes Angela.'

'Director CE to see you sir.'

'Thank you,' and Miles Thompson, the Head of the British Intelligence Directorate, got up from his chair by the windows overlooking the Thames and dropped the two-page, classified log sheet, which he had been reading, in his in-tray. 'Morning Michael, take a seat,' and the Director indicated an armchair opposite the one he had just vacated.

'Morning Miles; not good news about Nigel Lucas,' Michael Carrington replied taking the offered seat.

'I was reading the overnight log from the Operations Centre. What family is there?'

'He wasn't married. Hardly any of my field operatives are . . . . much the same as those in E Directorate. Parents are divorced and his father was killed in a road accident last year. He has a sister who's a civil servant in the Home Office. I should have a copy of the police report when I get back to my office. All I know at this stage is that he was killed by a single shot from a 12 gauge shotgun at point blank range. I shall be visiting his mother later today.'

'I gather the Foreign Secretary asked us to supply a minder for this VVIP gathering of Diplomats on the Granvil Estate.'

'His outer office contacted my CE4 Diplomatic Protection and spoke to Fiona Ransby.'

'Did they specify any threat?'

'Fiona said 'no' when I asked her that, but they muttered vaguely about the possibility of some hugely significant deal or contract in the Middle East and they feared that this gathering of

Ambassadors at a function where everyone is armed could attract unwanted interest from any element wishing to obstruct the deal.'

'Correct me if I'm wrong, but Nigel Lucas, despite his anglophile name, could pass anywhere as an Arab.'

'He could and has been exemplary in the work he has done for CE1 with counter terrorism. He not only looked the part but spoke a slack handful of Arabic dialects, Urdu and Pashto. We moved him across to CE4 only a month ago to give him a rest.'

'Was he shooting?'

'Oh yes. Anyone not shooting would have stuck out like sore thumb at what is probably one of the best and most expensive shoots in England. The only ones more expensive are the grouse shoots in the Borders and Scotland.'

'Silly to speculate at this stage, but is there any possibility that this could be a case of mistaken identity?'

'That's one of many lines Fiona's guys are working on right now.'

'Is there going to be another of these VVIP shooting parties?'

'Next Saturday; the deal which the FCO struck with the Duke of Cranborne consisted of two days; one for all the Ambassadors to familiarise themselves with the routine and etiquette and then the main event a week later when they can host their Prime Ministers who will be in this Country for a meeting of the G20 Nations. The day's shooting is a key feature of their entertainment package.'

'And now there's no minder?'

'That's the problem. Because the current terrorist threat level is 'severe', and probably ought to be 'critical', every one of the CE1 teams is working round the clock. Nigel was available because we had moved him across to CE4 . . . .'

'You want to task an operative from E Directorate?'

The Director CE nodded.

'That makes sense because if this plot to obstruct whatever might happen in the Middle East develops and goes abroad then the assignment would rightly come under E. Do you have anyone in mind Michael?'

'We need someone who's familiar with game shooting in this Country, who speaks Arabic and is at ease in such VIP company.'

'Ability to speak Arabic probably more important than shooting . . . .' but Miles interrupted.

'Not sure I agree with you there. How much did Nigel know about game-shooting?'

'Very little.'

'That may or may not have contributed to his death.'

'I don't suppose John Gunn would be available?'

The Head of BID smiled. 'He's taken a few days leave, but I'll have a word with David.'

'Many thanks Miles,' and Michael Carrington got up and left the Director's office.

*

The midnight-blue Jaguar XKR was cruising sedately along the D671 south of Châtillon-sur-Seine on on its way to Calais. Gunn had spent a week of his leave in Monte Carlo staying with a long-standing friend who was now a successful Formula One racing driver. It had been a very relaxing week of gastronomic suppers both ashore and on yachts of various degrees of luxury and parties which went on long into the small hours of the morning. He had managed not to lose too much money on the Black Jack and Roulette tables in the Casino and was now indulging in one of his favourite hobbies, driving along the by-ways of France stopping for lunch and staying overnight in whichever small auberge or hotel took his fancy. His Blue-toothed cellphone rang. He pressed the 'receive' button on the steering wheel.

'Yes.'

'You're needed back in the office, John.' He recognised Angela's voice—the PA to the Director of BID.

'How urgently?'

'ASAP . . . can you give me an ETA?' Gunn glanced at his watch.

'Ten hundred tomorrow . . . . acceptable?'

'That's fine . . . . please come straight to the boss's office.'

'Will do,' and he broke the connection. He then punched 'Calais' followed by 'quickest route' into the Garmin satnav which directed him onto the autoroute A26 round the east of Troyes. He let the Jaguar eat up the miles to Calais which it did effortlessly.

At the ferry check-in he had to pay an administrative fee as he was on an earlier boat than previously booked. He then drove on following the signs to the lane number he had been given at check-in. He found the lane and joined a queue of cars already waiting for the ferry. The woman at the check-in had told him that it would only be a half-hour wait before they started loading the cars. A long autumn day was just turning from dusk to dark as Gunn got out of the Jaguar to stretch his legs. There was now another queue beside the Jaguar.

He became aware of raised voices coming from the front of the queue on his right and then saw a woman hurrying along the queue of cars, bending down at each driver's side window to say or ask something. Gunn pressed the 'lock' button on his key fob and walked up the line of cars to investigate. Whatever the woman was saying to the people in each car, there appeared to be no response. Gunn wondered whether she was asking for help or offering a warning. Whatever it was, there was absolutely no response 'so perhaps she's asking for money,' Gunn conjectured. 'There's nothing more likely to switch off the majority of Joe Public than a beggar.' In the unflattering sodium light of the concourse, he recognised the 'woman' as one of three young girls in a cabriolet Mini he had overtaken some fifty miles back on the A26. They had waved cheerily as the sleek Jaguar with UK plates had overtaken them. At that moment the girl looked up and saw Gunn.

'Oh, can you help us please?'

'What's the problem?' Gunn asked.

'There're two men in the car ahead of us in the queue who were jossing us. We thought it was all in fun until they grabbed Julie's i-phone an' now won't give it back. We've asked lots of people to help . . . .'

'But no luck,' Gunn finished for her. 'OK, let's go and see if we can get them to give it back.'

'Oh thanks so much,' and she hurried back to the car with Gunn following her.

The car in front of the Mini was a 'day-glo' orange Suburu with a tailpipe of vast dimensions resembling a drainpipe. 'Nice bit of metal, but usually driven by no-brainers,' Gunn muttered as he tapped on the driver's window which had been quickly raised as his approach was spotted. Barely six inches in front of the Suburu was a black Range Rover. A single middle finger was raised at Gunn. He smiled and walked back to the girl driver of the Mini.

'Hi there,' Gunn smiled at the girl. 'Please drive forward until your bumper is touching the one in front. Put the handbrake on and the car in first gear. Got that, luv?'

'Yes, OK,' and the car eased forward until it touched the Suburu which was now pinned in by the Mini and Range Rover.

Gunn returned to the Suburu and removed a small Swiss Army knife from his pocket. He opened the gadget for removing stones from horses' hooves and bent down by the off-side rear wheel. He had purposely selected the wheel which was in full view of the driver's wing mirror. It would allow him to wrench the door open if the driver started to get out. The valve dust cap came off quickly and the inserted penknife gadget produced a loud hiss of escaping air. A stream of muffled foul language erupted from the driver who could do nothing to move the car as he was blocked in front and rear, but it produced the exact result for which Gunn had hoped.

The driver's door was flung open and the man started to get out, but got no further. Despite his hedonistic week in Monte Carlo, Gunn had lost none of his agility. He grabbed the driver's right wrist, bent it back until the man screamed in agony and then heaved him out of the car, spun him round and slammed him against the bonnet of the Suburu where three very hard blows with a partially clenched fist knocked him senseless. Gunn removed an unpleasant little kitchen devil knife from the man's left fist. Before the man in the passenger's seat realised what was happening, Gunn reached in, grabbed a handful of his shirt and heaved him out of the car through the driver's door.

'The i-phone please.'

'It's in the car,' was said sulkily.

'Then get it,' and Gunn picked the man up and rammed him head-first back into the car which reeked of cannabis, but still kept hold of the waistband of his trousers. A hand came back holding the phone. Gunn took it.

'Is this yours?' The girl nodded and took the phone.

Gunn pulled the man out of the car. He then took out his wallet from the back pocket of his chinos and removed the Metropolitan Police ID which he held in front of the man.

'If either of you causes any more trouble I'll have the Dover police meet us when we dock and both of you will be arrested . . . . oh, and I suggest you pump up that tyre or change it for a spare.'

*

'Morning John, how was Monte Carlo?' Miles Thompson greeted Gunn as he was shown into the office of BID's Director. Gunn had joined BID at almost the same time as Thompson when the latter was the Director of the Espionage Department. Also in the office was the recently promoted current Director of E Department, David Simpson and Michael Carrington, the Director of CE Department.

'As glitzy as ever, sir,' and Gunn sat in the proffered armchair.

'I've called you back a couple of days early because there's an assignment for which you are particularly suited,' and Miles then explained what had happened at the Granvil Estate shoot the previous weekend. 'Did you know Nigel?'

'Yes, very well. He was a great help when I was learning Arabic. We had many an evening together while I was struggling with the Arabic script. That's a damn shame. Has his sister been told?'

'Yes, and his mother,' Michael Carrington replied. 'The funeral was yesterday.'

'And the assignment, sir?'

'I want you to take Nigel's place at the same shoot this Saturday. On this occasion it's the Prime Ministers of these countries as well as their Ambassadors. How's your shooting?'

'Not too bad . . . . I went to the West London Shooting Centre about a fortnight ago. I hit most of the clays, but missed a couple of fast left to right crossers.'

'Your own gun?'

'A trusty AYA box-lock ejector which I've had for nearly ten years, Gunn replied.

'Do you know the Jardine family?'

'Know of them, but never met any of them.'

'Good . . . . you are on loan to CE and Michael will give you the full brief which he will do right now unless you have any questions.'

'No questions, sir,' and Gunn left the office with Michael Carrington.

*

Once they were seated in the CE Director's office with coffee provided by his PA, Louise, Gunn's briefing for the assignment began. The Director handed him a sheet of photocopied foolscap.

'Just scan this letter from the FCO for a moment and then I'll tell you what I was told by the Duke's elder son, Richard, or the Marquess of Purbeck to give him his full title.'

'Is the family very title conscious?' Gunn asked.

'No . . . . just the opposite so I'm told. The younger son is Andrew or Lord Corfe and the daughter is Cecile or Lady Cecile. Neither the family nor the staff at Granvil Hall uses the titles or the official form of address for a Duke and his family. You'll find all that background in the brief which Louise has prepared for you.'

'That's refreshing. Does the brief include details of how this shoot is run?' Gunn asked as he glanced at the names on the FCO letter.

SHOOT

UNCLASSIFIED—SENSITIVE

Protocol Department
Foreign and Commonwealth Office
King Charles Street
London SW1A 2AH

Telephone: 020 7008 1500

7 October 2012

HOSPITALITY FOR VISIT OF FOREIGN HEADS OF GOVERNMENT AND UK HEADS OF MISSION SATURDAY 12 OCTOBER 2012

This is the amended and final list of those Heads of Government and their UK Heads of Mission who will attend the Granvil Estate Shoot at the invitation of His Grace the Duke of Cranborne on Saturday 12th October 2012.

The escorting officer throughout this visit is Mrs Linda Gwyn-Jones who can be contacted on her mobile phone: 07984 509824.

Saudi Arabia
HE HRH Prince Mohammed Bishara, Second Deputy PM
HE HRH Prince Mohammed bin Hadad, HOM

Kuwait
HE Mr Sabah Al-Abadi, Prime Minister
HE Mr Maloof Al-Dahar, HOM

Qatar
HE Mr Rashid Al-Shadid, Prime Minister
HE Mr Nahas Al-Shamoun, HOM

UAE
HE Mr Mohammed Said Al-Nazari, Prime Minister
HE Mr Rahman binMansour Al-Rahal, HOM

Pakistan
HE Mr Wasem Halabi, Prime Minister
HE Mr Hassen Nassar, HOM

Jordan
HE Mr Sarkis Al-Samaha, Prime Minister
HE Mr Said bin Shadid Al-Shamoon, HOM

Oman
HE Mr Mustafa bin Seif Al-Khouri, Prime Minister
HE Mr Amari bin Naifeh Al-Nader, HOM

Bahrain
HE Mrs Pamela Handal, Prime Minister
HE Mr Quereshi Shammas, HOM

There will be four FCO hospitality officers:

Mr Michael Douglas-Smith
Ms Cala Williamson
Mr Eric Lustgarten
Mr John Gunn

BE Grey-Newton LVO
Head of Protocol
Room 2301

UNCLASSIFIED-SENSITIVE

'Yes it does. Miles has told me how much you enjoy your game-shooting so you'll know much more about this than me. I gather from the Duke's son, Richard, that the shoot is licensed . . . . and covered by insurance, for twelve guns to shoot on any one drive. The Heads of Mission and their Prime Ministers will take it in turn to shoot. The four FCO hospitality officers . . . . of which you are one and another is a woman . . . . will shoot on every drive.'

'Were the three FCO officers on last week's shoot?'

'Yes, together with Nigel.'

'Do we have any background on those three? Sorry, perhaps it's in the brief.'

'Just a moment,' and Michael Carrington buzzed his PA. 'Louise, does the brief provide background material on the three FCO officers who were on last week's shoot?'

'No sir, just their mobile numbers.'

'Thank you,' and the Director released the switch on the intercom. 'We should have covered that, John, but any particular reason you need it?'

'The woman—Cala Williamson; Cala is an Arabic name. It means 'castle', so I'm particularly interested in her background, how she acquired her very English surname and for which department she woks in the FCO.'

'That's an oversight on my part,' Carrington admitted.

'Could Louise get our Research Centre to do a very thorough dig into their backgrounds.'

'Of course.'

'OK, I've got all that, sir, so what's the thinking behind Nigel's death?'

'All of the countries represented on that shoot are, generally speaking, pro-West.'

'Pakistan?' Gunn queried.

'Generally,' the Director conceded with a smile. At the moment it seems that the murder of Nigel was either a case of mistaken identity or he saw, heard or discovered something which sealed his fate.'

'Questions?'

'Yes, of course.'

'Did Nigel look like one of the Heads of Mission?'

'Yes he did . . . . the Pakistani Head of Mission, Mr Hassen Nassar.'

'How many beaters were there?'

'Twenty, five of whom were women; they did all the picking-up of the birds with their Labradors and Retrievers. All of them were regulars and all have confirmed to the police that no stranger joined their ranks on any of the eight drives either before or after lunch. Which reminds me, lunch apparently, is a very splendid affair; 'field of the cloth of gold' with priceless silver and crystal. That may well be an area worth checking as it's a mixture of an up-market catering company—'Aristocaters', would you believe—and the Granvil Hall catering staff.'

'OK, one more question before I go and study the brief. Has the FCO given us any hint of what this meeting of Middle East Diplomats is all about when only Saudi Arabia of the eight countries on this list is a member of the G20?'

'All that the Head of Protocol—Grey-Newton—would say is that the FCO believes that some big deal . . . contract, call it what you will, is in the offing. The FCO has never forgiven Thatcher for depriving their Embassies and High Commissions of MI6 officers during the creation of BID. You will know that they were replaced with BID selected and vetted independent, in-country agents, known only to the Head of Mission and Defence Attaché. It wasn't stated, but I was left in no doubt of the intimation that had the FCO had its own agents in its Embassies it would be better informed.'

'Many thanks, sir: I will now go and study Louise's brief.'

CHAPTER 2

Gunn walked back to his mews house in Elm Park Lane and spent the rest of the afternoon studying the brief. There was very little to be gained from the information about the Diplomats, except their names. There was even less to be gained from the very meagre information on the three FCO officers. Michael Douglas-Smith was a Second Secretary in the Political Department. Eric Lustgarten was a Third Secretary in the Economic and Consular Department and Cala Williamson was a third Secretary in the Overseas Trade and Investment Department.

'Presumably the Protocol Department did a trawl around the various departments to find officers with some experience of game-shooting and it's associated safety procedures and who owned their own guns,' Gunn surmised to the empty drawing room where he was reading the brief. On an impulse, he went to his study and thumbed through his address and phone number card index. He dug out the card for the Research Centre on the 14th Floor of Kingsroad House and jotted down the number of Samantha Fox, the Head of Research.

'Yes John, what can I do for you,' came from a cheery Samantha.

'Oh hi! Sam, have you been tasked by CE to do some research on the Diplomatic shooting party next Saturday?'

'Doing it right now.'

'Any chance of giving me some details in advance on the three FCO officers?'

'Yes, any one in particular?

'Cala Williamson first and then the two men.'

'Thought you might be interested in her. The report will be on Michael Carrington's desk by end of play today, but here comes a preview: Cala Williamson was Cala Nassar before she married Clive Williamson. She is the only daughter of Hassen Nassar, the Head of Mission at the Pakistan High Commission in Lowndes Square. The marriage lasted just over two years and they divorced when he was posted back to London on completion of his three year tour as a Third Secretary in the Management Section of the British High Commission in Islamabad. There are no children. Cala achieved a good degree at Princeton University in New Jersey and with her acquired British Nationality would have had no difficulty getting a job at the FCO. She is a keen sportswoman and was a 'possible' for the Pakistan trap shooting team at the 2012 Olympics.'

'Thanks Sam, that's really helpful . . . and the two men?'

'Douglas-Smith is a graduate from Birmingham University where he was Head of the Student Union. He is now a Second Secretary in the Political Department of the FCO. He's single, leaning noticeably to the left in his political views and, surprisingly, lists game and trap-shooting as his favourite sports.'

'And the third guy?'

'Lustgarten, minor public school education followed by good degree from St Andrew's University and now on his first appointment in the Consular Department of the FCO. He's been game-shooting for many years on his father's farm in Oxfordshire. Any more?'

'No that's great, many thanks, Sam.'

'Take care John . . . why not come and have a coffee in our little empire.'

'I'll take you up on that, thanks again,' and Gunn ended the call.

The next morning Gunn was up early, completed his run, shower and breakfast of croissant and coffee by 8am and walked into the EDS/BID building in Cale Street just after 9am. His BID card let him into the secure lift area where he joined other BID staff just as the lift door was closing. He reached across to the bank of buttons and pressed 14.

'Morning John,' Samantha greeted him as the automatic glass doors of the Research Centre closed behind him. 'You've saved me making a call to Director CE. Here's a copy of our research into the Granvil Estate shooting party—aristos, diplomats, peasants et al and here's that coffee I promised.'

'Many thanks, Sam . . . . I dropped by to ask you whether you had been able to dig up any background on the people associated with the three FCO officers . . . .'

'Particularly . . . .'

'Cala Williamson.'

'Beat you to it, John. After we spoke yesterday afternoon, I thought I might run her name past our guys in Counter Terrorism. The Assistant Director, Barry Windsor, put my call through to Mohammed Abbas Beg.'

'And?'

'And he told me that Cala Williamson came onto CE1's radar about four months ago because she was seen in the company of an Iranian asylum seeker, Ghalib Malouf.'

'And CE1's interest in Malouf?' Gunn queried.

'Remember the three men convicted back in March for a terrorist bomb plot?'

'The report yes, but not the names.'

'Irfan Khalid, Ashik Ali and Irfan Nassar.'

'Once again that name appears . . . . her brother?'

'Mohammed thought that he might well be a cousin, but it indicates that Miss Williamson has been keeping some very suspect company since her arrival as a divorcee in this country.'

'Most useful, Sam; any further additions to your background search?'

'No that's it.'

'Many thanks,' and Gunn finished his coffee and left the Research Centre, called in at Louise's office and collected his copy of the background search and walked back to Elm Park Lane. On arrival at his mews house, Gunn switched on his laptop and

Googled 'The Plough' pub in Lower Shalford. From the brief he had learnt that the pub was the focal point of the village. Obediently Google displayed the pub's home page which told him that the pub had four en-suite bedrooms. He dialled the number and booked himself into a double room for two nights from that evening. That would give him a chance to have a good look round the village and listen to the bar gossip in the evenings.

Decision made, Gunn then went into the garage, unlocked the steel security cabinet and removed his 12 gauge, side-by-side Spanish AYA shotgun. Having cleaned and oiled the gun, he then put together the bits and pieces he would need for a day's shooting—gun sleeve, cartridge belt, two boxes of cartridges, game bag . . . . he paused, 'no, no need for that,' he muttered, as all the game would be picked by the dogs and carried in game bags by their owners. He went up to his bedroom and packed a bag with the clothes he would need, wrote a note to Mrs Charlesworth, who watched over him and the house like a mother hen, and then loaded everything into the boot of the Jaguar. His last task was to phone Carrington's PA, Louise, and inform her of his plans.

Gunn left London on the M3, joined the M27 (West) north of Southampton and turned off onto a 'B' road when the motorway ended. He nearly missed the sign to Lower Shalford which took him onto a narrow country lane with thick hedgerows on either side ending in Lower Shalford's village green. The Plough was on one side of the green together with a cricket pavilion. On the opposite side was an attractive church with a square Norman tower. The other two sides of the square were occupied by picturesque and 'extremely expensive cottages,' Gunn muttered, as he parked the Jaguar at the back of the pub. He glanced at his watch; 5.30. He left his backpack, bag and gun in the boot and went into the pub. Early evening it might have been, but there were already a dozen or so people in the bar. As a total stranger to the village, his arrival caused a momentary lull in the hum of conversation as heads turned in his direction. The obligatory buxom village barmaid put down the glass she was drying and came over to Gunn.

'Yes sir, what can I get you?'

'Nothing to drink at the moment thanks, but I've booked a room here . . . .'

'You'll be Mr Gunn, just a moment sir,' and she reached under the bar and produced the room register which she opened and turned towards Gunn. 'It's room one, up the stairs and first door on your right and those are the keys. Will you be having supper here tonight?'

'Yes please; I have a shotgun with me. Do you have a room or cabinet where it could be locked away?' Gunn had mentioned the gun quite quietly, but it proved what a bunch of eavesdroppers and gossips were in the bar because all conversation ceased as though turned off by a switch.

'We do, sir; I'll put it in the cabinet with the landlord's gun. He's out at the moment, but I expect he'll want to see your shotgun licence. Don't worry about that lot,' and she nodded towards her clientele. 'We had a bit of an incident here this last weekend on the Duke's estate. Some poor fellow was killed in a shooting accident. We've had the police around here for the last few days . . . . makes everyone a bit nervous.'

The buzz of conversation had returned, but now there was no pretence of surreptitious eavesdropping, Gunn was now the focus of attention in the bar.

'Will you be shooting on the Granvil Estate, sir?'

'Yes, I understand it's one of the best in the country.'

'The landlord, Arthur, my husband, oh and I'm Liz . . . .'

'John,' Gunn offered.

' . . . . would agree with that,' as they shook hands over the bar. 'He does the beating for the shoot.' There was a pause while Liz served another customer and then returned to Gunn. 'So you'd be from the Foreign Office to look after all these embassy people, I expect, sir?'

'No, Liz, I'm from the Intelligence Directorate . . . . BID. It'll be my job to make sure there're no more accidents.' Gunn had decided that the quickest way of finding Lucas's killer would be to make himself the killer's next target, hence the decision to go to the gossip centre of the village and give them all something to talk about.

'So you're a sort of secret agent Mr Gunn.'

'Sort of, Liz, but now not so secret,' Gunn joked.

'Do you need a hand with your bags?' Liz offered.

'No thanks, I'll go and get my things from the car and then take up your offer of that drink,' and Gunn left the bar and returned to the Jaguar. 'That should stir things up,' Gunn thought, as he removed his backpack, bag and gun from the boot. He slung the pack over one shoulder, the sleeved gun over the other and carried the bag into the pub and up the stairs to his room. After he had unpacked his bag and pack, he took the gun downstairs where he was met by a cheerful, rotund, red-faced and bald-headed man.

'I'm Arthur, your landlord, Mr Gunn. Liz tells me you have a shotgun you would like locked away.'

'John . . . . yes please,' as they shook hands.

'Let me take it and I'll show you where my gun cabinet is.' Gunn handed over the shotgun and followed Arthur along a passage which led to a utility room filled with washing machines and tumble dryers, outside clothing, boots and a steel gun cabinet. The landlord produced a key from his pocket and opened the cabinet which had four foam rubber slots, one of which was occupied by an over-and-under shotgun. The gun was placed in a vacant slot and the cabinet was locked. 'Here you are, sir,' and he handed the key to Gunn. 'I'm the only person who has the other key for this cabinet.'

'Thank you, Arthur, can I buy you a drink?'

'Don't mind if I do, sir,' and the two men went back into the bar where Gunn bought two pints of Bass. Gunn had only taken one sip of his beer before his plan seemed to bear fruit. A very overweight man with a florid complexion who had been sitting with another group beyond the far end of the bar picked up his beer and walked over to join them.

'Evening Arthur, mind if I join you?'

'Not a bit Stan,' and the landlord turned to Gunn.

'John, Stanley Tullet, one of the regular beaters on the Granvil Estate; John Gunn, who'll be shooting on the Estate on Saturday.' The two men shook hands.

'Couldn't help hearing you tell Liz you're from BID. Arthur's told you I'm a beater on the Estate. That was a nasty business last week. Man who got shot . . . . Lucas. Was he one of your lot?'

'Yes, he was from BID,' Gunn confirmed.

'I was hoping to have a word with the police as it's just possible I might have heard something during the lunch break on that day. I didn't think much of it at the time as we were all concentrating on making sure we did a thorough job.'

Although he had his back to a group of four people—two men and two women—sitting in a booth, Gunn saw one of the women get up from the table, abandon her unfinished drink and leave the pub. Stanley put his beer down on the bar and wiped his forehead with the back of his hand and then continued with some difficulty.

'It was only later . . . . after the discovery of the body in Huntsman Copse that I remembered the conversation I'd overheard, but the constable . . . I spoke to . . . didn't . . . . seem interested . . . .' Stanley's last few words choked in his throat and he gasped, holding onto Gunn's arm for support. Beads of perspiration ran down his forehead. Gunn grasped the man before he collapsed and lifted him across to an empty booth.

'Dial 999 for an ambulance and the police,' Gunn said urgently over his shoulder to the landlord while he eased Stanley off the seat in the booth, lowered him onto the floor and began to pump his chest with both hands. Gunn heard someone say that he was going to get the doctor and after what seemed an age, but was only two or three minutes, he was relieved by the local doctor who took over the CPR until the ambulance arrived. Everyone stood back as the paramedics from the ambulance entered the bar. The paramedic felt for a pulse in the gamekeeper's neck. He shook his head. The body was placed on a stretcher and taken out of the pub and into the ambulance.

CHAPTER 3

'Tetrodotoxin is probably the most lethal poison known to man,' DCI Nesbit announced to the assembled clientele of the Plough. Everyone in the pub had been told that they would have to stay there until statements had been taken. Gunn noticed that this imposition appeared to cause no anxiety as he suspected that the majority would have stayed in the pub until closing time. DCI Nesbit had asked Liz Lumsden, the landlord's wife, if anyone had left the pub in the ten minutes before Stanley Tullet had collapsed. She confirmed that only one person, Mrs Cox, had left the bar shortly before he collapsed, but no one else had entered or left the bar.

'Mr Tullet was declared 'dead on arrival' at Felbridge Hospital,' the DCI continued. 'I've just been told by the hospital that the poison which killed him is not the sort of stuff you buy over the counter in *Boots*. It comes from only two known sources; the puffer fish—or Fugu—to give it its Japanese name, and the blue-ringed octopus. Both of these are native to Japan and Australia, but are unknown in the seas around us in the UK.'

'I'm telling you this because the poison takes effect within two to five minutes of ingestion or contagion.' The DCI studied his police notebook. 'It can be administered by injection, by mouth or just contact with bare skin. There is no antidote to the poison which causes asphyxia, paralysis and finally cardiac arrest. The cause of death gives all the symptoms of a heart attack. It's quick and extremely painful as you have all witnessed. We . . . . that is the police . . . . were fortunate that the doctor in triage at Felbridge A and E has done a stint in London's Hospital for Tropical Diseases. But for that, a killer might have got away with murder. The landlady has told me that Mr Tullet and all of you have been in the bar for the last twenty minutes. That means that there is every chance that his killer is in this bar listening to me now.'

'We've divided you into two groups; Detective Sergeant Finch will take statements from all of you at that end of the bar,' and DCI Nesbit pointed to the far end of the bar, 'and I will deal with this group.'

'This group' consisted of three of the four people in the booth behind Gunn, the landlord, his wife Liz and Gunn. The two men and one woman in the booth told the DCI that Mrs Cox had left the pub suddenly because she remembered that she had left a cake in the oven. They all told the DCI that they had seen nothing out of the ordinary from the time Tullet had picked up his beer and moved from the far end of the bar to join the two men at this end of the bar. The landlord and his wife confirmed their account. He then turned to Gunn.

'I don't believe you live in Lower Shalford, sir?'

'That's right, Chief Inspector, I'm staying at the Plough for a couple of nights and shooting on the Granvil Estate on Saturday. I work for the British Intelligence Directorate and am replacing a colleague of mine who was killed last Saturday.'

'Mr Lucas?'

'Yes.'

'May I see your BID card, sir?'

'Of course,' and Gunn showed him the card.

'Thank you, sir. Are you the only officer from BID attending this shoot?'

'Yes, Chief Inspector,' and Gunn replaced the card in his wallet.

'May I have a word outside, sir?'

'Sure,' and Gunn followed the DCI out of the pub.

'Is there anything that you would like to add to what was said in the bar?' the DCI asked as they paused outside the pub.

'I think just two things, Chief Inspector. When Stanley Tullet came over to the landlord and me he said that he thought he had some information about Lucas' death. It was after he said that, Mrs Cox got up and left the pub. The only other thing that struck me was that the poison which killed him might have been put into some of his pills if he was self-medicating himself—diabetes or high-cholesterol or whatever. I have to say that Tullet looked like a heart-attack waiting to happen without the assistance of that unpronounceable poison. That would mean that his killer could be anywhere and not necessarily amongst the pub clientele.'

'Thank you for that, sir. If you do pick up any more gossip, I'd be grateful if you could pass it on to us.'

'Yes of course.'

'And take care; two deaths are two too many, we don't want a third, sir,' the DCI warned Gunn.

*

Gunn awoke with a start. He glanced at the luminous figures on his watch; 2.27. He had set the silent vibrator alarm on his mobile phone for 2.30, but had woken a couple of minutes early. He cancelled the alarm. 'Was it just the usual thing of his brain pre-empting the alarm, or had something else alerted him?' he wondered, as he lay in the pub's comfy double bed. Used to the constant night time level of sound of life in London, the complete lack of it in the village of Lower Shalford meant that the slightest noise was audible. There it was again . . . . a floorboard creaking? . . . . door hinge squeaking? . . . . or foot-fall on the uncarpeted tread of the stairs? Gunn slid out of bed and quickly dressed in jeans, cotton polo-neck sweater and trainers. He removed the Glock 26 automatic from under the pillow and pushed it into the waistband at the back of his jeans.

He carefully unlocked his bedroom door and eased it open slowly. There it was again . . . . a sort of scraping noise, like a mouse scratching at the wainscoting. Gunn locked his bedroom door and then tested the first tread of the stairs, placing his feet on the side of it where the timber frame of the staircase would be more rigid . . . . no creaks, but more scratching, sounding like metal against metal rather than a mouse's claws against wood. Three more treads to the bottom of the stairs . . . . a slight creak from the last tread! The scratching stopped instantly. Both Gunn and the scratcher, whether human or animal, were listening with bated breath. Slowly, slowly, Gunn released his breath and let the final tread take his full weight. One step down and he would be in the corridor which led from the front door of the pub through to the back door and utility room via the landlord's gun cabinet.

C r e a k! The noise from the ancient oak floorboards at the foot of the stairs mimicked that of a Hammer horror movie exaggeration of a vampire's coffin lid being raised. Gunn swung round the balustrade at the foot of the stairs into the corridor, all attempt at stealth abandoned. Light filtered through the back door glazing from the outside security light at the back of the pub. Silhouetted for a brief moment against this dim light was a bulky figure standing by the gun cabinet. As Gunn moved towards the figure it disappeared down the corridor with remarkable agility and out of the back door. He followed as far as the yard at the back of the pub where all the barrels, empty bottles and gas cylinders were stacked. As the figure escaped from the yard, the neatly stacked metal beer barrels were overturned, cascading over the yard, making a horrendous din and very effectively blocking any pursuit by Gunn. He returned to the back door where the landlord, in pyjamas, was standing, holding a shotgun.

'Did you see who it was?' a natural question in the circumstances from the landlord, but pretty pointless, Gunn thought, as he'd only been in the village a few hours.

'No Arthur, I couldn't even tell if it was male or female . . . . whatever the sex it was a fairly large and bulky intruder, or someone who had disguised their size for their night time prowling,' Gunn answered, as he picked his way through the beer barrels, trying not to cause any more noise.

'Bloody man . . . . or whoever . . . got the gun cabinet open,' Arthur swore. 'It's a five lever lock and I'm sure that there are only two keys.'

'It was open when you took that gun out?' Gunn asked.

'Yea, I always keep a couple of cartridges in the draw of the bedside table on my side of the bed.'

'Could you very carefully hand that gun to me please? No! Don't break it open and unload it, although I appreciate your safe practice.'

'OK . . . here you are . . . . what's the problem John?'

Gunn took the shotgun from Arthur and pushed the top lever over with his thumb. With his left hand on the stock-piece and right holding the butt at the neck, Gunn 'broke' the gun open, revealing the brass percussion ends of the two cartridges which Arthur had inserted into the chambers. By the light of the halogen security lamp, Gunn carefully removed first one and then the other cartridge, which he handed to Arthur. He then raised the tip of the barrels towards the security lamp and with one eye closed, looked up the barrels.

'Thought so,' Gunn muttered.

'What is it?'

'Have you got a wooden cleaning rod?' Gunn asked.

'Sure . . . . back in the gun cabinet,' and Arthur disappeared through the back door to reappear moments later carrying the wooden cleaning rod. Gunn inserted the rod into the muzzle end of the top barrel until it would go no further. He then pushed more firmly and slowly the rod went down the barrel until a 12 gauge cartridge fell from the chamber. Gunn picked it up.

'This is a very deliberate act of attempted murder, Arthur. Look at this cartridge and Gunn showed him the brass percussion end of it. 'The rim of the cartridge has been filed off so that it would go through the chamber into the barrel. If you had fired this gun, the explosion would have blown your head off. The lower barrel is just the same.'

'Bastard!' was all Arthur could say.

'He or she is certainly that, but let's check the other gun,' Gunn suggested, heading back into the pub followed by the landlord. Both guns in the cabinet had been sabotaged in the same way. Gunn removed the rimless cartridges out of the barrels and then handed back the original gun to Arthur. 'When did you last fire this?'

'Just this morning, John; I went pigeon shooting with Bob Simmons, one of the gamekeepers on the estate.'

'Close the breech and then pull the triggers, one by one . . . . I know it's not good for the firing pins to do this without sleeper cartridges in the chambers, but humour me please.' Arthur closed the breech and then barely touched the trigger for the top unchoked barrel, when there was a very audible click of the firing pin striking.

'Fucking hell!' Arthur swore, 'that's not even a hair trigger. The gun would have gone off if I had just touched the fucking trigger. Now I see why you didn't want me to unload before passing the gun to you. What's been done to the gun?'

'Whoever did this certainly knows his way round shotgun firing mechanisms. Stop me if you know all this.'

'No, go ahead, I want to know what this bastard is up to.'

'When you break the gun open it cocks the gun by compressing the firing pins on their springs. They are held in position by the sear . . . .'

'Sear?' Arthur queried.

'It's a small hooked-shaped piece of metal which interacts with the trigger. If you like a hair trigger, a gunsmith can engineer the sear to suit your shooting style. In this case I reckon our night visitor adjusted it so that it was barely retained by the trigger. That must have taken him some time even if he is an expert with gun mechanisms. Oh yes, and he either has a key to your cabinet or our visitor is also an expert lock-picker. Do you have a local gunsmith?'

'Yes, Nat Breakspear; shop on the other side of the green. He makes a fortune from all the wealthy visitors to the estate. Sets up shop each Saturday at the shoot lodge.'

'I suggest we pay him a visit tomor . . . .' Gunn glanced at his watch, 'today, and get our guns checked.'

'Good idea; I'm off back to bed . . . . oh, I nearly forgot, I owe you one John.'

*

Gunn waited until he heard the landlord's bedroom door close and then let himself out of the front door of the pub. There was no street lighting, only the occasional security light on some of the properties surrounding the green. He wasn't sure what prowling around in the dark would achieve, but some years of experience with BID had taught him that a quick follow-up to an event such as the break-in to the pub sometimes yielded a successful result. Gunn paused to recall the sequence of events as the intruder made his getaway. Gunn had decided for the time being that it was a 'he' not a 'she'.

After leaving the back yard of the pub, he had kept going in a straight line—roughly, Gunn reckoned, which meant that he hadn't turned right across the front of the pub, but had gone to the left—at least, initially. 'Right, to the left it is,' and Gunn set off along the hedgerows of the properties near the the pub. There was no ambient light from an overcast sky with no moon or stars which made him almost invisible in his dark clothing. He reached the edge of the green. Continue round the green or take the road which led out of the village? Gunn opted to go on round the green. He had gone about fifty yards when he picked up the unmistakable smell of smoke from a French cigarette . . . . Gitanes or Gauloises? The latter, he thought, which had the more astringent smell.

Gunn wet his finger and held it up. What wind there was appeared to be coming from the garden on his left. He walked along the head-high hedge until he came to the gate into the front garden of a cottage. It was so dark that it was hard to tell whether the building was 'house' or 'cottage', but Gunn's eyesight was now accustomed to the dark. He removed the Glock automatic from the waistband of his jeans, sank to a crouch and edged forward to the gate. The source of the cigarette smoke was immediately apparent. On the gravel path leading up to the front door of the cottage was a smoking cigarette butt. Barely half of the cigarette had been smoked, indicated by the half inch of ash still attached to the glowing tip. Right beside the butt, the gravel had been compressed by several large foot imprints.

'Either a female with abnormally large feet or a man,' Gunn thought as he rose to his feet. 'Someone stood here, probably watching the pub, and if he had night glasses he would have seen me leave the pub by the front door. I reckon he's only been gone a minute or so, but would have waited here to see if a sabotaged shotgun had exploded or to see if anyone was going to follow him. That's enough night time prowling. Our intruder tonight is someone with large feet who smokes French fags and is an expert with shotgun firing mechanisms . . . . oh yes, and can pick locks.'

CHAPTER 4

'Morning Arthur,' a pause, and then, 'morning sir,' as Gunn followed the landlord into the gunsmith's shop. Arthur introduced Gunn to Nat Breakspear as the two shotguns were carefully laid on the counter.

'Strange business in the pub last night,' the gunsmith continued, 'my Margaret's gone round to spend some time with Stanley's Edna. A rum old business, as I said already, what with that deadly fish poison an' all.'

'Rum's the right word Nat. John here and I need some advice. John's here from BID to help with the security up at the estate for tomorrow's shoot. Last night we had a break-in at the pub. Someone tampered with these guns by forcing a cartridge beyond the chamber and adjusting the triggers so that the slightest pressure would release the firing pins.'

'Bloody hell! What's going on Arthur?' Nat's indignation and incredulity seemed genuine enough, so that probably ruled him out as the pub intruder, Gunn decided. He had been watching the gunsmith closely.

'We don't know, but first of all we need these guns checked out by you . . . . John's side-by-side first please. Before you do that John wants to know how long it would have taken to tamper with these guns and who would have the skill to do it in the semi-darkness of the corridor where I keep my gun cabinet.'

'For a skilled gunsmith in good light, five minutes max . . . . don't spread that around Arthur or I'll lose my livelihood,' Nat added with a conspiratorial wink to the landlord.

'You always have overcharged, you bugger!'

'Like you and your best bitter in the pub,' was the instant rejoinder. 'An inexperienced person would take double that time.'

'How many people in this village would be able to do that,' Gunn asked.

'Certainly all the gamekeepers on the estate could have done that, and, of course, Richard Jardine, the Marquess. He's a damn good shot and knows his guns. As far as I know there are fifteen guns owned by people in this village . . . . could be more, but that's the total that bring their guns to me for an annual overhaul.'

'Last question, Nat, before we leave you to fix the guns; do you know anyone in the village or up at the estate who might do something like this?' Gunn asked.

'No sir, I don't,' was the short reply.

*

'The gunsmith business seems to be doing well for Nat in Lower Shalford,' Gunn commented after the door had closed behind them.

'Yes, I think he does alright,' Arthur replied slightly vaguely.

'How many other people in the village can afford cars like that Porsche Cayenne SUV parked behind his shop?'

'Oh, he does better than that John. There's a 911 Turbo-charged Porsche in the garage at the back of the house.'

'So where does all the money come from Arthur?'

'Mainly, I expect, from the very wealthy clients that jet here in private charter aircraft from all over the World to shoot on the estate. Nat has a direct line to Purdey and Holland and Holland and gets a right royal commission for every pair of guns he persuades the Duke's clients to buy.'

'What would a matched pair of Purdeys cost?'

'Oooh, anything from £40,000 to £150,000.'

'For some reason he's not telling us all he knows. 'Might have been better, Arthur, if you had been on your own. The BID tag might have made friend Breakspear less than fully cooperative.'

Before the landlord could reply his cellphone rang. It was his wife Liz.

'We have another reservation at the pub, John; a woman arriving this evening. Would that be from BID?'

'No, she'll be one of the Diplomatic Service hospitality escorts for the VIPs on the shoot. She'll have a shotgun.'

'No problem, there's enough space in the cabinet, but I'm not sure how I prevent another attempt to tamper with the guns. Any ideas?'

'We know that the intruder can pick locks and is mechanically adept so even if you installed a new cabinet it wouldn't stop another attempt, if the intruder is determined to have another go. I suggest you tell her to keep the gun in her bedroom.'

'OK, I'll do that. Now it's time to take you up to the Granvil Estate,' and the two men returned to the pub where they got into the landlord's Mitsubishi Shogun and headed for the Duke of Cranborne's Granvil Estate.

*

'John Gunn sir; John's from the Intelligence Directorate and staying at the Plough,' was the landlord's introduction of Gunn to Richard Jardine, Marquess of Purbeck.

'Richard Jardine, John; dreadful business last week with Nigel Lucas. He was also from BID. Did you know him?'

'Yes sir, very well and his family,' Gunn replied. The Duke's elder son was a shade under six foot, well-built, fair-hair receding at the temples and blunt, unaristocratic features and dressed in jeans, polo-neck sweater and gumboots.

'I'm very glad to have you here as it's vital that the shoot tomorrow is a success for all these high value ministers and diplomats. My father spoke with Sir Miles yesterday. You come with quite a reputation John, so very glad you're batting for us. I'll leave you with John Hamden, my gamekeeper, who'll show you around and explain the programme for tomorrow,' and so saying the Marquess climbed into a battered Mini-Moke jeep and disappeared up the drive to Granvil Hall.

'I'm sure you're very busy,' Gunn had turned to John Hamden, the gamekeeper, 'but if you could spare the time to show me where Mr Lucas was found and give me a rough idea of the programme for tomorrow, I will then get out of your hair.'

'Yes Mr Gunn, hop in that Landrover and we'll start at Huntsman Copse. Arthur, I suggest that you stay here with Barry. We won't be long.' Gunn was joined in the Landrover by the gamekeeper and his black Labrador.

'We both share the same first name and I'm very happy for you to call me John if that suits you,' Gunn offered as they drove off to Huntsman Copse.

'That's fine by me,' but the rest of the drive to the copse was in silence.

There was a track leading into the copse which was used by the shoot keepers to top up the bowser which provided the pheasants with a constant supply of fresh water. John Hamden turned onto the track and stopped by the fenced enclosure. The pen was full of birds, the majority of which were this year's poults as they seemed fairly small to Gunn. It was as though the gamekeeper had read his thoughts.

'We try and persuade the guns to leave the small birds, but the majority of them can barely tell the difference between a magpie and a pigeon, let alone undersize and mature pheasants; you a shooting man, John?' he asked as they both got out of the Landrover and walked over to the area of disturbed ground in the bracken where the body of Nigel Lucas had been found. The blood-discoloured bracken and earth provided clear evidence that it was the place where Lucas had been shot and bled out.

'Yes I am, but I can't afford more than two or three days in the season. Can you think of any reason why Lucas would come here?' and Gunn continued before the gamekeeper could answer, 'it must have been to meet someone or because he knew . . . . or had discovered that other people were going to meet here. What's the routine on these shoots?'

'On our weekly shoots, all the guns arrive on the day and depart at the end of the day's shooting. But it's different for these VIP days.'

'How different?' Gunn asked.

'Well, all the VIPs come down the evening before . . . . mostly by helicopter from London. There's a big do in the Hall that evening, a traditional shooting breakfast the following morning and lunch in that marquee you saw at the shoot lodge. We do four drives in the morning and four after lunch. It's a mystery to me how they hit any birds in the afternoon after the amount of wine and port they drink at lunch. The helicopter comes at five to collect all those who wish to return to London.'

'What's the security like in Granvil Hall for the VIP's guns?'

'Every one of the guest bedrooms has its own secure steel cabinet. The key to that cabinet comes with the key to the bedroom.'

'Do they all shoot on every drive? I'm sure the police have asked all these questions already, so please humour me.'

'That's no problem and the police haven't asked any of these questions . . . . that is, not as far as I know. They may have asked the Duke or his son, the Marquess, but they haven't asked me or my assistant keepers. To answer your question, no, they don't all shoot on every drive. There are sixteen VIPs and four minders; there are twelve guns on each drive—eight VIPs and you four, then the VIPs swap over for the next drive. If Mr Lucas had not been on his peg,' the gamekeeper paused with eyebrows raised in query.

'Yes, it's OK John, I'm up to speed on peg numbering. What do they add each drive?'

'Four; so they draw their shoot card on arrival from the reception desk set up in the grand lobby of the Hall and the number on that shoot card is their peg for the first drive. The diplomats shoot on the first drive and the PMs on the second and so on.'

'So if Lucas wasn't on his peg, you or one of your keepers would have spotted the missing gun immediately?'

'Immediately; it's more than my job's worth to miss something like that.'

'And the gunsmith, Breakspear; is he of great value to the shoot?'

'Other way round, the shoot's of great value to him. All the wealthy shoot clients know Nat Breakspear and most arrange to buy their guns through him. No, Nat does alright John. The Duke's policy is to support local people and small businesses.'

'This is my last question . . . . for the moment; why did no one notice that Lucas hadn't left after the shoot?'

'He came down by train to Felbridge, taxi from the station to the Plough and taxi again the next morning to the Hall. He just had a backpack with some changes of clothing and his side-by-side shotgun in a short leg-o-mutton sleeve.'

'The backpack and gun?'

'The pack we found at the lodge the next morning after the discovery of the body; the gun is still missing.'

'Bonus last question?'

'Of course.'

'I want you to imagine that you're the person who used the shotgun to blow off Lucas's head . . . .'

'Steady . . . .'

'No, really this will help. You're standing here,' and Gunn picked up a stick and positioned himself where Lucas's feet had been. 'And you blow his head off at point blank range, like so—bang!' and pointed his imaginary shotgun at the place where the bloody mass of brain matter, bone and tissue had been.

'How do you know that's how he was shot?'

'If he'd been standing up his head would have been blown all over this area. It wasn't; what had once been his head bled out on that spot.'

'Yea . . . . alright I agree with that. So what was the question?'

'Come here and swap places with me.' John Hamden obliged and took the stick from Gunn. 'Right now, you've just shot Lucas. The sound of the shot could well bring unwanted attention for you so you must get rid of the shotgun quickly. Would you get rid of it here or hide it under your shooting jacket and get rid of it later?' The gamekeeper played the imaginary role well pointing the stick at the bloody stained patch of bracken and then looking up as though he could hear someone coming. He looked all round . . . . at the pen, the bracken and then the trees and then last of all, the water bowser.

'I know what I'd do,' he said walking up to the bowser. 'I'd take off that large round filler cap on the top of the bowser and drop the shotgun inside.'

'Let's take it off and have a look.' Now enthused, the gamekeeper removed the six inch diameter filler cap and turned on the tap.

'I'll get a torch from the Landrover. It'll only take a couple of minutes to drain.' As the last of the water drained out of the bowser, the gamekeeper climbed on to it, unscrewed the filler cap and shone his torch into the empty bowser.

'Eureka! I spy one shotgun.'

*

'That was a brilliant bit of detective work finding the shotgun. DCI Nesbit will be very envious.'

'Luck; it also convinced me that John Hamden had nothing to do with this business. Arthur, would you mind if I use you as a sounding board to try and make sense of what I've learned so far,' Gunn asked, as they drove through the Granvil Estate in the landlord's Mitsubishi.

'No, go ahead, John; it's what the detectives do in all the TV police soaps. I'm told it's either to help or confuse viewers about the identity of the murderer.'

'At BID's training centre we are taught how to be very effective criminals . . . . lock-picking, safe breaking, explosives, unarmed combat, firearms, forgery and so on, but no techniques of detective work. That's left to our colleagues in Counter Espionage. OK, so this is what I've found out so far. Last Friday, all the diplomats arrived by helicopter at 6.15 in the evening. The two men from the FCO travelled together in Eric Lustgarten's Fiat and stayed the night with his parents in Minstead. They weren't invited to the pre-shoot dinner on the Friday evening, but drove in the same car the next morning to the shoot. Cala Williamson drove down in her sports car and stayed in your pub on the Friday night, as did Nigel Lucas.'

'Yes, that was odd. He arrived by taxi from Felbridge at about 6 and asked me to book a taxi for him the next morning at 8 to go to the shoot. He didn't have supper in the pub and didn't come into the bar. The taxi arrived just before 8 and I unlocked the gun cabinet and gave him his gun. He didn't have breakfast. Ms Williamson didn't get to the pub until just before ten that Friday night. She didn't come into the bar, but went to her room after I'd locked the gun away. She did have breakfast the next morning and left the pub at about 8.30.'

'So what was odd?'

'Well, it seemed as though they purposely avoided each other.'

'Did Lucas know that Cala was going to the shoot?'

'Yes, because I told both of them that there was another member of the shoot staying in the pub.'

'Yes, you're right, that is odd, but we've now established why no one noticed that Lucas hadn't left Granvil Hall. When I was shown the spot where he was found this morning, a couple of other possibilities struck me. Lucas had his head blown off while he was lying on his back in the bracken.'

'How do you know that, John?' Arthur asked as he waited for the electric gates of the estate to open.

'Had he been standing up . . . . or sitting for that matter, the blood spray would have gone everywhere. It didn't. It was all in one tight area where his head had been. I don't think he was killed by a shotgun. I think he was shot in the head by a rifle or handgun and then his own shotgun was used to blow his head off to hide the evidence of the weapon used to kill him. Incidentally, I didn't mention the bit about another weapon to the gamekeeper.'

'Jesus! This gets more and more complicated by the minute. So where does poor old Stanley Tullet come into this?' Arthur asked as he pulled into the Plough car park. The two men stayed in the car.

'Do you know anything about Stanley's background?'

'A bit; Stanley was born in Pakistan in 1948, just after partition with India. His father worked on the railways, as did many Brit ex-pats. The family didn't come back to this country until the sixties just before one of the conflicts with India.'

'Did he speak Urdu?'

'Oh yes, and Hindi, he was invaluable on the pub quiz team for any question connected with Pakistan or India.'

'This morning, before I had breakfast, I rang our Operations Centre in London. I wanted to know how quickly that Tetrodotoxin would take effect. If it had been put in Stanley's beer or into one of his Statin capsules, it would have taken at least five minutes to have the effect that it did have when he was talking to me. If it been administered any other way, it would have been more like twenty minutes.'

'Which means?' Arthur asked.

'That the poison was administered before he told me that he had some information and Mrs Cox's rapid exit from the pub had nothing to do with her overhearing that I was from the Intelligence Directorate or that Stanley wanted to tell me something. It's highly unlikely, I believe, that Stanley's pills were doctored in the pub last night. I reckon his pills were doctored some time during the shoot—possibly at lunch—because the murderer had discovered that Stanley spoke fluent Urdu and had probably overheard a conversation which the conspirators had assumed no Brit would understand.'

'Which would seem to point the finger at the Pakistani High Commissioner,' Arthur volunteered as he opened the car door.

'Possibly,' but Gunn did not add that it fitted the information he had learned from Sam in BID's Research Centre about Cala Williamson and the company she had been keeping.

CHAPTER 5

A police car pulled into the pub car park as Gunn got out of the Mitsubishi. DCI Nesbit got out, almost before the car stopped and without closing the car door, strode over to Gunn and Arthur.

'Don't think he's going to kiss you on both cheeks, John.'

'You could be right Arthur.'

'I've just been told by the gamekeeper that you found Lucas's shotgun. What were the two of you doing at a crime scene?' the DCI challenged. With a discreet hand motion, Gunn signalled to the landlord not to react to the challenge. Gunn said nothing.

'Well . . . . haven't you got anything to say?' a severely stressed DCI demanded.

'Chief Inspector, I will tell you how the shotgun was found when you've calmed down. It was not a crime scene because you had already declared that it was no longer one, so anyone could go there. I will do everything I can to be of assistance to you without interfering. I have enough sense not to try and be a 'Miss Marple'. You need to find one or perhaps two murderers; I need to discover the implications of these murders on international relations between the UK and the countries represented by their Prime Ministers at the shoot tomorrow. Now do we have a deal?' There was a pause. The DCI's shoulders sagged and he appeared to age about ten years in as many seconds.

'I'm sorry, John. I've been harassed all morning by the Assistant Chief Constable. I should be old enough and wise enough not to let it get to me. Our Chief Constable is in a flap too. Someone only has to mention that the Duke of Cranborne is involved and the Chief goes ballistic. Now that we have all these very important people arriving this evening in an area where there have been two murders, it's a miracle that I haven't been relieved of authority in this investigation in favour of them. Let me start again; that was a thoroughly commendable piece of detection and I'm really grateful for your help.' Gunn turned to the landlord.

'I'll catch up with you shortly, Arthur.'

'First pint's on me,' and the landlord tactfully withdrew to the pub.

'I'll do everything I can to help your investigation, but I'm not even from the Counter Espionage Directorate of BID and so have none of its specialised training and liaison with your SO15 Counter Terrorist Command. BID trains me and my colleagues in the Espionage Directorate to be expert criminals, so let me reassure you that there is no way that I will dabble in amateur crime detection. Having said that, do you have the result of the post-mortem on Lucas?'

'Yes I do, was there any particular aspect that you wanted to know?'

'Amongst the bloody mess of brain and bone that had once been Lucas's head, did your pathologist either find a bullet or any indication that his head was first hit by a bullet before his own shotgun was used to obliterate the evidence.'

'She did and with all honesty I can say that was because I asked her to check that possibility. What aroused your suspicions?'

'Because it seemed to me that he had bled out on the spot where he was found, it followed that the murderer must have been standing over him when the shotgun was fired at point-blank range. If Lucas had been standing when the shotgun was fired, the blood spatter would have gone everywhere.'

'Well spotted, now I'll buy you that pint that Arthur was offering.'

'Thanks, I'll take you up on that; what calibre?'

'Nine millimetre,' and the two men walked across to the pub.

*

'There are three garages at the back. I'll leave the Mitsubishi out so put the Jaguar in the end one on the right. Here, this is the garage key,' and Arthur handed Gunn the key. They had agreed that the landlord would not mention to Cala Williamson that Gunn was also going to the shoot.

'Too many coincidences, Arthur; she's the daughter of the High Commissioner, she's mixing with extremists, she was present on the last shoot when Lucas was killed and she knows how to handle a gun.'

'Liz has just taken a call from Ms Williamson who's on her way here. She asked what time we finished serving supper. Liz told her 9.30 and she said she hoped to be at the pub by nine if the traffic got no worse.'

Gunn was chatting to the landlord in the bar of the Plough. It was now just after 8.30 on that Friday night and the bar was filling up with clientele. Gunn took a sip of his pint of Bass and then left the bar to garage the Jaguar out of sight. When he returned to the bar, the landlord told him that Cala Williamson had arrived in a small black Mercedes sports car. His wife, Liz, had taken her up to her room.

'She's in number 2, opposite your room,' the landlord told him. Only a few minutes later Cala Williamson came into the bar. Tall for a woman from the Asian sub-continent, raven black hair and a curvaceous figure, she caused most of the male heads to turn.

'Drink before you have supper, Ms Williamson?' the landlord offered.

'A Bloody Mary, Arthur; I'll be sitting over there,' and she waved in the general direction of the seats and booths.

Gunn watched her out of the corner of his eye. She went to a table that was occupied by two men. One got to his feet as she reached the table and the other man stepped aside and moved over to a group of three men at another table. Arthur poured the Bloody Mary and added the Worcester and Tabasco sauces.

'Who's the large guy she's sitting with, Arthur?'

'That's Alec Moore, one of the assistant gamekeepers on the Estate; fancies himself as a bit of a ladies man. He used to work at a small engineering company in Minstead until he was sacked after numerous allegations of indecent assault from female colleagues in the company.'

'Did he go to court?'

'No, the story is that he was given the option—get out or go to court. Alec chose the easy option—as usual and left the company. I'll just deliver this to her high and mighty self . . . . back in a minute.'

Gunn finished his pint, left the bar and went up the stairs to the bedrooms. He tried the door to number 2, but it was locked. Gunn went across the corridor to his room and removed two items from his back pack before returning to the door of number 2. With the aid of the first item from his pack, a lock pick, he had the door open in a matter of seconds. He locked the door behind him. There was a small, smart Louis Vuiton case and matching carry-bag on the bed. Hanging in the wardrobe was an exceptionally smart Jaeger lady's shooting outfit. There was a washing bag and bits and pieces of make-up in the bathroom—nothing hidden inside the lavatory cistern. Thrown on the bed was a gossamy scrap of negligee which would purposely conceal nothing and there was nothing of interest in the case or bag.

'Oh well, if not here then possibly in her car,' Gunn muttered under his breath, just as a key was inserted into the door lock. The door handle was turning as Gunn stepped inside the wardrobe and pulled one of the doors shut, leaving the other side with Cala's shooting outfit open, as it had been when he entered the bedroom. Gunn could see nothing. He could only judge what Cala—if it was Cala—was doing by listening. The muffled footsteps on the carpet went across to the en-suite bathroom. Gunn risked a peek from his hiding place. The lavatory was flushed, but as he ducked back into the wardrobe he had just enough time to see an automatic lying on top of the negligee where it had been dropped as Cala went into the bathroom.

The footsteps came out of the bathroom and paused by the bed and then came to the wardrobe. There was an aroma that seemed alien to Cala. Gunn waited for the door to open. A hand came into the wardrobe holding the automatic which was pushed into the pocket of the shooting jacket. The footsteps went across the room to the door. The door opened and closed and a key turned in the lock. Gunn removed the automatic from Cala's shooting jacket and stepped out of the wardrobe. He was a holding a small 9mm SIG-Sauer, 9 shot automatic. He left Cala's room, locking the door behind him. Once back in his room, he removed the magazine and worked the top slide on the automatic which ejected the round from the chamber. He completed the disassembly of the automatic, pushed up the safety catch and pulled the trigger, exposing the firing pin. He then used the second implement—the file on his multi-tool Gerber—to file down the firing pin until it could no longer strike the percussion cap in the base of the bullet case. That completed, Gunn returned the automatic to the pocket of Cala's shooting jacket and went downstairs to the bar.

'That's the one I said I'd buy you,' Arthur greeted Gunn's return to the bar as he placed a pint of Bass in front of him. 'She's gone through to the dining room with Alec. They seem to be very good friends.'

'French cigarettes!'

'What about them?' a rather startled landlord asked.

'Does Alec Moore smoke?'

'Yes,' and then more confidently, 'yes he does . . . . those foul smelling French cigarettes; why?'

'I believe that we know the culprit who broke into the pub last night and tampered with our guns. People who smoke transfer the smell of tobacco to other people. I was nearly caught by our friend Cala while I was in her room just now. I couldn't place that smell until I came back to the bar.'

'I could have given you the pass key . . . . saved you a bit of trouble,' Arthur offered.

'Certainly not, otherwise you would have been implicated in my search of her room.'

'Useful?'

'Very, I might just have stumbled on the weapon that really killed Lucas, but now comes the difficult bit; why?'

'It seems to me that both your man and Stanley either saw something or overheard something. Something that was so incriminating that they had to be silenced.'

'Agreed, but what? The weak link in this is the assistant keeper, Moore. Was he in here last night when I let it be known that I was from BID?'

'Oh yes, he's in here every night and usually the last to leave. He's married' . . . . then came a pause while Arthur served one of his clientele . . . . 'and two children; really nice kids.'

'So he'll have told Cala that I am the replacement for Lucas. I'm certain that he's last night's intruder. He would have no reason to fix our shotguns unless he was paid to do it or was receiving other favours for his cooperation.'

'The latter, John: bet your life on it. That man's got a permanent short circuit between his brain and his bollocks. When the latter's engaged the former is useless. He'll be shafting that Pakistani lady like there's no tomorrow. He'll be like putty in her hands. Yes Barry, what'll it be . . . usual?' as Arthur turned to serve a man who had just come to the bar.

'Aye Arthur,' and the man placed the exact change on the bar.

'Barry, this is John. He'll be on your shoot tomorrow. It was his friend who was killed last Saturday.' The two men shook hands.

'Nasty business that, John. Close friend of yours?'

'Yes he was. Any objections if I ask you some questions about that?'

'No, none at all . . . . you a sort of detective?'

'Sort of; can you remember if at any stage Stanley Tullet was close to the Pakistani High Commissioner for whatever reason?'

'Aye, you'll see how this works tomorrow. We have lunch after the fourth drive. Before lunch we all have a drink together . . . . keepers, beaters, guns and his Grace, the Duke usually joins in. His Grace reckons it's good for the posh guns to mix with us peasants,' Barry added with a chuckle. 'I expect Stanley wanted to talk with the Pakistani guy to show off his knowledge of the country and whatever language it is they speak. The Pakistani guy was talking to that woman who's with Alec in the dining room. Someone said that Alec got his leg over her during the lunch break. Where was I . . . . oh yes, Stanley must have been standing quite close to them for quite a few minutes, waiting for the right moment to introduce himself. I was then called away by John . . . . that's John Hamden the head keeper . . . . to go and fix one of the guns with Nat . . . . he's our gunsmith.'

'That's most helpful . . . . and Mr Lucas?'

'I met him of course, but no, I didn't see him talking with anyone in particular, but at the end of the shoot I did see him set off in the direction of Huntsman Copse. Someone said he'd gone to look for something he'd dropped on the last drive . . . . Huntsman Copse was the last drive of the day.'

'Again, very helpful. Can I get you another of those.'

'Aye, thanks John.' Barry Foxton picked up his pint of mild and bitter and headed back to the table where he had been sitting before he came up to the bar. Arthur came back to Gunn's end of the bar after serving some of his clientele.

'I said Alec's brainless when he's sniffing around some bitch on heat, but even he will realise that as you nearly caught him red-handed last night, the means of putting you out of action has failed. I'd bet a night's bar takings that he was also the one who tampered with Stanley's pills. She would have to be the person who put him up to that. I mean where would Alec get hold of that poison? And coming to think of it, as he failed last night, what's to say he won't have another go tonight?'

'That thought hadn't escaped me Arthur. I think you'll be OK. The only reason he tampered with your gun was because he didn't know which one was my shotgun.

*

It was a few minutes after ten when Gunn went up to his room. He locked the door behind him and went over to the window to draw the curtains. Below him at the rear of the pub, he just caught a glimpse of Cala and Alec walking in the direction of some parked cars. Gunn left the curtains, unlocked the door and went out of the pub by the back door into the yard. He then went round to the back of the pub where he had seen Cala and Alec. There were only two cars, the landlord's Shogun and a black Mercedes GL series, seven-seater estate car which was heaving up and down on its suspension as Cala Williamson and Alec Moore took part in vigorous post-prandial exercise.

Gunn returned to his room, drew the curtains, locked the door and placed a chair under the door knob. He retired to bed still wearing his jeans and a T-shirt. It seemed barely minutes later that he awoke. Someone had tested the door to see if it was locked. Then came a 'click' as something was inserted into the lock. Gunn slid off the bed, pushed the pillows under the duvet to take his place, put his Glock automatic into the waistband of his jeans and tip-toed over to the door where he carefully removed the chair to one side. The door knob turned and the door opened slowly. Again, the unmistakable smell of Gauloise cigarettes preceded Alec Moore's move into Gunn's room. Gunn wondered if the sexually satisfied Cala would be in the corridor as back-up with her modified SIG-Sauer automatic. That was a risk he would have to take. He removed the Glock from his jeans and holding it by the slide and trigger guard, back-handed it with all his strength into Alec's face. There was a howl of pain as blood spurted from Alec's broken nose. Gunn grasped a handful of his thinning hair, spun him round and pushed him out of the room. Alec staggered into the corridor, lost his balance at the top of the stairs and fell head first down the flight to the hallway below. Gunn went down the stairs followed by the landlord complete with shotgun. Arthur turned on the lights in the hall.

'Can you phone for the police and ambulance,' Gunn asked the landlord as he knelt down beside the inert form of Alec. Gunn felt for a pulse. 'He's unconscious, but with some pretty serious injuries.' Alec's right hand was firmly clenched. 'Do you have any rubber gloves and a plastic bag Arthur?'

'In the kitchen, I'll get them,' and having made his call to the emergency services, Arthur disappeared into the kitchen. He reappeared with a pair of yellow rubber gloves and a Tesco plastic bag. 'Any good?'

'Yes, those'll do fine.' Gunn pulled on the gloves and then prised open Alec's clenched right hand. 'Thought so,' he muttered.

'What is it?' Arthur asked bending down to get a closer look. In Alec's unclenched hand were the remnants of a broken glass phial, blood and some colourless fluid. Gunn pulled the plastic bag over Alec's hand to prevent anyone inhaling any fumes from the poison.

'The biter bit; I'll bet a pint of your best bitter that's Tetrodotoxin which was intended for me,' Gunn answered as the police 'blues and twos' could be heard in the distance.

CHAPTER 6

Even at half past one in the morning, it didn't surprise Gunn that the first person through the door into the pub was DCI Nesbit. Pressurised by his own Chief Superintendent at Felbridge and the Chief Constable at County Headquarters in Winchester, the DCI was determined that he would be the first person on any crime scene associated with the Cranborne Family and the Granvil Estate. He arrived just as the paramedics were trolleying Alec Moore on a stretcher out to the ambulance. Gunn explained what had happened from the arrival of Cala Williamson to Alec's attempt to break into his bedroom. The landlord corroborated Gunn's version of events the previous evening when questioned by the policeman.

'But no sign of Ms Williamson?' DCI Nesbit queried.

'Since supper last night, not a sign of her. I can't believe that she could have slept through all the noise. Shall I go and check her room?' Arthur Lumsden offered.

'Yes please . . . . just a second Mr Lumsden,' and the DCI called over a WPC from one of the police patrol cars. 'Morrison, please go with the landlord up to Ms Williamson's room and ask her to get dressed in some warm clothing and come down here.' The two of them disappeared upstairs while DCI Nesbit went back over some of the events leading up to the attempted break-in to Gunn's room.

'What made you suspect Mr Moore?'

'A number of things; I learned today from Barry Foxton—he's another of the Estate gamekeepers—that Stanley Tullet, who's a fluent Urdu speaker, had overheard a conversation between Cala

Williamson and her father. The subject of that conversation must have been so sensitive that there was only one course of action; Tullet had to be silenced. Cala had already identified Moore as a gullible 'lady's man'. According to the landlord and his fellow beaters she had seduced Moore during the lunch break last Saturday . . . .'

'Where, for God's sake?' the DCI interrupted.

'In the Huntsman Copse—that's the nearest pen to the shoot lodge. Barry Foxton and a couple of beaters with their dogs had volunteered to 'dog-in' some birds who were out in the open feeding off the grass seed.'

'Dog-in?'

'Yes, before beating an area to drive the birds towards the guns, dogs are used to push the birds back into the cover, whether it's a field of kale, copse or whatever.'

'Thanks, I'm more at home on the streets of London than this huntin', shootin', fishin' lark. So what happened?'

'I don't have the lurid details, but they caught Alec and Cala 'in flagrante'. From that moment on he was like putty in her hands. Here's the landlord.'

'She's gone. Bed not slept in,' Arthur Lumsden announced, as the DCI was called on his cellphone. He answered, thanked the caller and turned to Gunn.

'Alec Moore was dead on arrival at A and E.'

*

Struggling with a full English breakfast prepared by Arthur for the two of them, they heard the arrival of the two chartered 8-seat Eurocopter 155s as they flew over the pub to land on the wide gravel forecourt in front of Granvil Hall.

'That'll be the VIPs arriving for their traditional English hunting breakfast,' Arthur commented pointing towards the ceiling of the pub breakfast room with his knife.

'The Duke certainly gives his guests value for money,' Gunn said, finishing his plate of bacon, eggs, kidneys, hash-browns, sausages and grilled tomatoes. 'Those two choppers must set him back at least £20k.'

'You're right, he is generous, but he gets a whacking great grant from the FCO, so it's you John and I and the rest of the taxpayers who help to foot the bill for this day's shooting.'

Gunn finished his coffee and was about to go and collect his backpack and gun when a thought stopped him. 'I should have thought of this before, Arthur. Was Stanley sitting with any of his fellow beaters on Thursday evening, before he came over to talk to me?'

The landlord paused on his way to the kitchen with their empty plates. 'Yes, he was with Jeremy Cox and George Akehurst . . . . the three of them usually meet up in the bar most evenings . . . . especially on quiz nights.'

'Will they both be there today?'

'I'd put money on it. Do you want to meet them?'

'Yes I do; there's just a chance that Stanley might have told them what he'd overheard.'

'I should have thought of that. Follow me up to the Hall and I'll introduce you to them.'

'Thanks,' and Gunn collected his backpack and gun and walked out to the garage at the back of the pub.

*

Gunn followed Arthur's Shogun to the shooting lodge and parked up beside it. There was still an hour before the VIPs would arrive after their traditional hunting breakfast. Parked outside the front of the Hall were two Mercedes Unimog trucks. Arthur had told Gunn that these had been converted into really comfortable 10-seat all-terrain buses for the guns. The beaters were moved around in a tractor-towed, covered 4-wheel trailer with bench seats for 20. Other beaters were arriving as Arthur and Gunn joined a short queue at a kiosk serving hot coffee and bacon rolls.

'Thanks, I'll pass on the bacon roll after that mammoth breakfast,' Gunn declined the offered roll, but accepted the china mug of piping hot coffee complete with the Cranborne coat of arms.

'Right, come and meet Stanley's chums,' and Arthur led Gunn over to a small group of men, women and dogs. 'Jerry, George, I want you to meet John who was in the pub on Thursday evening. John works for the Security Services and is investigating Stanley's death. Only take a couple of minutes of your time.' The two men moved away from the other beaters with Gunn and Arthur.

'It's the police who are investigating Stanley's death; I want to find out what Stanley might have overheard in a conversation between the Pakistan High Commissioner and an FCO officer. This is connected with the death of one of my colleagues on last Saturday's shoot,' Gunn continued. 'I'd be really grateful for any scrap of information which you can remember, however odd it may have seemed and perhaps still does seem to you both.'

'Lovely man, Stanley was, had some great stories about his life in Pakistan. Wish they could hang the bugger who poisoned him. Do the police know who did it?' Jeremy Cox asked.

'They have some positive leads, but nothing yet which they can announce,' Gunn knew that patience would be required if he hoped to get help from the two men. George Akehurst had been silent up to this moment, but now butted in to Gunn's anodyne comment on police progress.

'Nice man that Lucas friend of yours. He spent some time with Stanley talking in that Pakistani language. Stanley was doing most of the talking. I expect that's what you want to know,' George offered.

'Was that conversation with Mr Lucas after he had overheard the High Commissioner's conversation?'

'Oh aye.'

'Did Stanley say anything to you at that time or in the pub last Thursday about that conversation?' Gunn persisted.

'Yes he did, didn't he Jerry?'

'Aye, it didn't make much sense to us, but what he was talking about last Saturday after the lunch break made more sense than what he was talking about in the pub on Thursday night. After we met in the pub, he said he'd forgotten to take his pills so he took them . . . . Statins, I think it were . . . with our first pint. It was only a few minutes before that poison . . . . if it was in his pills . . . . took effect.'

'Can you remember what it was he told you last Saturday?' Gunn asked. It was George Akehurst who answered.

'He said he couldn't understand why they were talking about 'eagles' . . . .'

' . . . . the birds?' Gunn interrupted.

'Yea, he said they were talking about moving these eagles to Afghanistan and he said that was odd because there aren't any eagles in Pakistan . . . . only buzzards and hawks.'

'He was sure that he'd heard 'eagles' and hadn't made a mistake?' Gunn queried.

'It was definitely 'eagles' weren't it Jerry?' George sought confirmation from his chum.

'Yea, it was eagles being moved from some place near Rawalpindi . . . . that was the place George, to Afghanistan . . . . two of them I think he said and then Stanley spotted your man, Lucas, and went over to speak to him. That was the last we saw of Stanley. We saw your friend Lucas during the afternoon drives, but Stanley must have gone home because we didn't meet up again with him until Thursday. He missed the pub quiz that Saturday night.'

'That was it?' Gunn tried to keep the disappointment out of his query.

'Yea,' both men said in unison.

'Many thanks guys, you've been most helpful,' and Gunn let the two men return to the group of beaters.

'What the fuck was all that nonsense about?' Arthur swore as soon as the two beaters were out of earshot.

'Makes no sense to me except the transport of something from Pakistan to Afghanistan which could be a consignment of weapons and/or explosives for the Taliban, but I know a man who knows a lot more about that part of the World than me,' and Gunn dug his cellphone out of his shooting jacket and pressed the speed dial.

'Catch up with you later,' and Arthur Lumsden tactfully moved out of earshot. Gunn acknowledged this with a wave as he was connected to the Operations Centre in Kingsroad House.

'Operations Centre,' Gunn recognised Terry Holt's voice.

'Going to secure speech,' Gunn said, pressing the 'secure' button on his phone.

'I need information quickly on a conversation which took place last Saturday between the Pakistan High Commissioner and his daughter Cala Williamson,' Gunn began.

'Roger to that, all this is recorded so tell me what you want and I will expedite immediately. Can I call you back?'

'Yes no problem,' Gunn confirmed, 'it seems that the entire conversation centred around moving eagles, I repeat eagles, and two of them, from somewhere near Rawalpindi in Pakistan to Afghanistan. The shoot starts in about half-an-hour so very grateful for any explanation.'

'Got all that. Get back to you asap,' and Terry Holt broke the connection. As Gunn put his cellphone back in his pocket, the two FCO officers arrived in a Fiat Uno and parked up by Gunn's Jaguar. He went over to them and introduced himself. 'John Gunn, Intelligence Directorate.' The three men shook hands.

'Dreadful business that with Nigel last week,' Eric Lustgarten sympathised as he removed his shotgun from its case and then added, 'have the police got anywhere with their investigation?'

'They're making progress . . . .' but Gunn's phone rang at that moment. 'Excuse me, and he walked out of earshot of the people gathering for the shoot and then answered the call. 'Hello.'

'Ops, John, secure please.'

'Roger,' and Gunn pressed the button.

'The Pakistanis have somewhere between 100 and 120 nuclear warheads ranging from 25 kilotons to 300 kilotons. They have more than adequate supplies of uranium and plutonium to make many more should they decide to do so. They also have a supply of Tritium which when added to a uranium or plutonium device increases its power by a factor of some 300%. The Country is not a signatory to the Nuclear Proliferation Treaty so there is no way of making an accurate assessment of its full capability. They have small warheads which can be delivered by air or large ones which are delivered by missiles of various sizes and range capability. The missile with the longest range at the moment is the Shaheen II at 2,500 miles—incidentally, shaheen is the phonetic English pronunciation of the Urdu word for 'eagle'. The missile technology and some of the hardware came from China but the nuclear expertise is home grown. There has recently been a considerable increase in Sigint coming out of GCHQ from that part of the world and the unconfirmed rumour is that a missile, or missiles, or a warhead may have been spirited out of the Country—possibly from Kahuta which is about 50 miles north-east of Rawalpindi or from Khushab in the north-west of the Tribal Area near the border with Afghanistan. The worst fears are that if true these missiles or warheads could be destined for the Taliban in Afghanistan. The current Prime Minister, Mr Wasem Halabi, has taken a hard line against the Taliban, which has made him popular with the West—especially the USA—but not so popular with the opposition and extremist elements in Pakistan which include the current High Commissioner in London, Hassen Nassar. Is that enough to keep you busy?'

'Thanks Terry, and for the speed of response.'

'Good hunting—drop by for a coffee if we're not in the middle of World War 3!' and Terry broke the connection.

'Oh shit!' Gunn swore aloud, but the only one to hear him as he walked back to the Jaguar was a black Labrador who was far too busy inspecting the backside of another Labrador to take any notice.

CHAPTER 7

As Gunn walked back to the two FCO officers, Cala Williamson's black Mercedes sports car arrived and parked on the other side of Gunn's Jaguar.

'That'll be Cala,' Michael Douglas-Smith remarked. 'Did you meet her John? I think she was staying in the Plough.'

'No,' Gunn answered truthfully, 'I did see her briefly yesterday evening, but I believe she spent the night elsewhere.' Another car arrived as Cala got out of her Mercedes in her immaculate Jaeger shooting outfit. The latest arrivals in an unmarked police car were DCI Nesbit and DS Finch. Cala removed her Beretta over-and-under shotgun from its case in the boot of her car, placed it in its slip and then walked over to the three men.

'Hi guys, you up for another competition to see who shoots the most birds?' and then with a commendable performance of acting which Gunn had to admire, 'oh sorry, I don't think we've met,' as Cala made a pretence of noticing Gunn for the first time.

'That's right; John Gunn, I'm BID's replacement for Nigel who was murdered here last week . . . .'

'Murdered! I understood it was a tragic case of suicide,' Cala interrupted with a display of shock and disbelief that would have convinced many, including her fellow FCO officers, Gunn judged.

'How awful! I thought he turned his shotgun on himself,' Eric added.

'That's what we were all meant to think. No, he was shot with a 9mm automatic and then his shotgun was used to blow his head off . . . . we didn't meet, Cala, but I saw you in the pub last night,'

Gunn added, turning back to her. 'Standing behind you are two policemen trying to look inconspicuous, who I suspect want to talk to you because witnesses in the pub said you were the last person seen with Alec Moore.'

'That's right, we had dinner together, before I left to stay the night in Felbridge. Why? Is there a problem?' The self-assured mask had slipped for a brief moment, but was soon restored.

'He died on the way to hospital in the early hours of this morning. Here's DCI Nesbit.' The policeman had walked over while Gunn was talking to Cala.

'Morning Ms Williamson, sirs, please don't rush away after the shoot is finished as I would like to speak to all of you,' and not waiting for any response the Chief Inspector returned to the unmarked police car where his Sergeant was speaking to Richard Jardine. The latter finished his conversation with Sgt Finch and then came over to the group.

'Morning everyone,' the Marquess greeted them cheerily, 'here are your cards,' and after checking the name on each card he distributed them. 'Same as last week . . . . you all move up four pegs on each drive, which means that you will all stay in the same relative position to the diplomats you start out with. Cala, you're on Peg 3, John—Peg 6, Michael—Peg 9 and Eric—Peg 12. Again, same routine, they have all been briefed by my father, but should you see any serious safety lapses, don't hesitate to take action . . . . with, of course, the utmost diplomacy! Any questions?'

'Could I swap pegs with John please?' Cala asked, predictably, as that would put her next to the Pakistani pair. Gunn guessed that DCI Nesbit had spoken with Richard Jardine which had resulted in Cala's separation from her father.

'No, sorry about that Ms Williamson. Any other questions?' There were none, so Richard Jardine hurried away to greet the arrival of the two Mercedes Unimogs bringing the diplomats to the shoot lodge. The beaters and dogs boarded the trailer and disappeared behind the tractor in the direction of Battle Firs, the first beat of the day. A long-wheel-base Landrover pulled up beside the four guns. The head gamekeeper, John Hamden leaned out of the driver's window.

'Hop in you guys and I'll take you up to the first drive. John, as the tallest, you'd better come in the front,' was added as he saw Cala heading for the front seat. They had gone no more than 100 yards when the gamekeeper's cellphone announced the receipt of a text message. 'Better check that,' and John Hamden stopped the Landrover as he read the text, 'looks like instructions from the boss.'

> *"Sy at the gate told shoot HQ Williamson arrived with male driver. Driver not on sy list. Only Williamson in car when it arrived at HQ. Show text to Gunn. Urgent"*

'Can you just hang on to this for a moment please,' John Hamden said, handing the cellphone to Gunn, 'while I drive. You might like to glance at the text, it's only about the start time for the first drive,' and he drove off.

Gunn glanced down at the text. 'Fine,' and cancelled the message only an instant before Cala leant over from the back seat.

'Any changes we need to know?' she asked.

'No, nothing major; one of the guns has left his glasses at the Hall so there may be a couple of minutes delay before the start of the first drive.'

'Right everyone, the wood in front of us is Battle Firs and there is peg number 1,' John Hamden pointed to the left side of the Landrover. 'Pegs 1 to 3 are on this side of the wood and 4 to 12 on the other side. Here's peg 3, Ms Williamson if you would like to jump out.' Cala got out and was handed her gun by Eric Lustgarten. The Landrover continued round the corner of the wood and stopped at peg 6. 'Can you two guys walk up to your pegs, I just want to discuss some security matter with Mr Gunn.' Both men in the back readily agreed, got out, collected their guns and started walking to their pegs. Once they were out of earshot, Gunn spoke.

'Do any of the drives have pegs which are really close to cover .... like a ride through a wood?'

'Yes, one, Witches' Wood—medium height fir and spruce with a ride through the centre; all the guns are in the ride—excellent snap shooting, but I doubt if our VIPs today will have much success,' John Hamden answered immediately and then added, 'the fourth drive and last one before lunch.'

'Would Cala know of that drive?'

'Oh yes, same routine as last Saturday which was a rehearsal for today.'

'After the third drive, can you arrange for one of your assistant gamekeepers to replace me?'

'Of course, it'll be Bob Simmons,' and after a pause while he did the maths, John added 'and that'll be peg 6 again.' He then got in the Landrover and headed back towards the shooting lodge. The two Unimogs arrived and following a well-rehearsed plan, one stopped in the middle of pegs 1 to 6 and the other went on to stop in the middle of pegs 7 to 12. The VIPs dismounted via a set of steps fitted to the back of each vehicle and each pair of guns walked to their assigned peg. Wasem Halabi, the Pakistani PM and his High Commissioner, Hassen Nassar walked past Gunn onto peg 7. If body language was anything to go by, Gunn judged, the two men could hardly be described as the best of friends. Gunn walked over to them, touched his cap and introduced himself.

'Good morning, Your Excellencies, I'm John Gunn; I work with the British Intelligence Directorate.'

'Wasem Halabi, and this is our High Commissioner Hassen Nassar. You have a very appropriate name for today's activity and for your job, Mr Gunn. I might have expected it to be James Bond!' was added with a definite twinkle in the PM's eye.

'No such luck, sir, but if I can be of any help during the course of the shoot, please let me know.'

'That's kind of you Mr Gunn. I gather that one of your colleagues met with an accident last Saturday and has since died. I am really sorry.'

'Thank you for that, sir.'

'My High Commissioner has a query. He is wondering why Ms Williamson is not escorting us. I'm sure you know that she is his daughter.'

'The detailed organisation has been the prerogative of the Marquess who is the Shoot Captain. Ms Williamson is on peg 3 hosting the Prime Ministers of Kuwait and Qatar. We all meet up at lunch, so His Excellency Mr Nassar will be able to catch up with his daughter then.'

'Thank you Mr Gunn, that is quite clear,' and then the PM turned to Hassen Nassar and switched to Urdu. The similarity between Urdu and Arabic meant that Gunn could understand the sense, if not the detail, of what was being said. The expression on Hassen Nassar's face said it all. Whatever was being planned by Nassar and his daughter, if anything, Gunn wondered, her position at peg 3 was unhelpful.

A blast on a hunting horn announced that the beaters were ready to start the drive. This was acknowledged by a whistle blast from the gamekeeper to indicate that the guns were in position and ready for the drive. Battle Firs covered an area of some ten acres on the crest of a hill. The guns were positioned in a semi-circle fifty yards from the edge of the firs and some 30 feet lower down. This meant that all the birds flying out of the Firs would be high ones and would require really accurate marksmanship by the guns to achieve a hit.

Gunn was paying only partial attention to the task of shooting any birds; the focus of this attention was directed at the two men on his right. He reminded himself that the sole purpose of his presence on the shoot was to prevent any attempt on the life of the Pakistani PM. If the other person in the car with Cala had been Ghalib Malouf—or whoever it was, Gunn rationalised—there was no chance of him making any attempt on the PM's life look like a shooting accident on this drive. If the gunman was hidden in Battle Firs, then all the guns would be out of lethal—human-killing— range from a shotgun. However, if the gunman was using a rifle then he could take his shot at the PM on any of the drives, but that would rule out any chance of passing off the assassination as a shooting accident. All of these possibilities flitted through Gunn's mind as the guns waited for the first flight of pheasants. In the distance Gunn heard the tapping of the beaters' sticks and the cackle of the disturbed birds.

The shooting started first on the edges of the drive as some of the birds flew out from the side of the Firs despite the efforts of the assistant gamekeepers vigorously waving their fluorescent yellow flags to drive the birds towards the centre of the semi-circle of guns. The cackling increased in volume and then with a furious whirring of beating wings the birds rocketed out of the undergrowth on the edge of Battle Firs. The Pakistani PM immediately displayed his marksmanship by taking a 'left and right', bringing down a brace of cock pheasants. Other guns were less fortunate and despite multiple shots, the majority of birds flew on, minus a feather or two, to live for another day. Gunn took a shot at a high bird, but missed. On his right, the Prime Minister had had considerable success and the dogs were busy picking up the birds he had shot. The beaters appeared on the front edge of the Firs and another blast on the hunting horn, followed by the whistle, ended the drive. Gunn unloaded his shotgun, re-sleeved it and walked over to the two men on his right.

'Well done sir, that was a most impressive display of shooting,' Gunn congratulated Wasem Halabi, the Prime Minister.

'Thank you, Mr Gunn, I am quite sure you would have had more success, if you had not been chaperoning us,' the PM generously offered on Gunn's inability to hit a single bird.

The Unimogs arrived and collected the VIP guns. John Hamden drove up to Gunn in his Landrover; Cala was already in the front seat.

'Next drive is Harold's Folly, then the Oaks followed by Witches' Wood which will be the last drive before lunch,' John Hamden announced as he let out the clutch and they drove off to collect the other two FCO officers. 'Ms Williamson, you are now on peg 7 for the next drive and Mr Gunn you will be on peg 10.'

The same routine followed on the next two drives. On Gunn's right the High Commissioner had very little success, only managing to 'prick' one young hen pheasant which was caught and retrieved by a Labrador and dispatched by its owner. On the Oaks drive, the PM repeated his success, proving that his marksmanship on the first drive was no fluke. On completion of the third drive, two Landrovers arrived as the Unimogs were gathering up the VIP guns. The second Landrover was driven by Barry Foxton with Bob Simmonds in the passenger seat. Once again, Cala was in the front passenger seat beside John Hamden.

'Mr Gunn, you're wanted at the Shoot Lodge. Bob will take your place on peg 6 for the Witches' Wood drive if you're not back in time. OK, hop in everyone and we'll get on with the next drive,' John directed as Bob joined him in the Landover and Gunn took Bob's place with Barry Foxton. Gunn caught a glimpse of Cala's face as the Landrover moved off; the expression was one of mixed anxiety and fury.

'I'll drop you off on the south side of Witches' Wood,' Barry said as he and Gunn headed off in the direction of the Shoot Lodge. 'The ride runs due east/west through the Wood. The beaters will line up on the north side and drive towards the ride. The wood on the south side of the ride is pretty dense, Mr Gunn. If anyone is hiding there, he will be very hard to spot.'

'Thanks for that, Barry. I'm going to leave my gun with you. I'll collect it at lunch.' Now out of sight of the other vehicle with the FCO officers, the Landrover swung away from the track leading back to the Shoot Lodge and pulled up close to the densely planted firs and spruce of Witches' Wood.

'No problem; take care Mr Gunn.'

CHAPTER 8

On the edge of the wood where the light and sun could reach the undergrowth, it was so dense Gunn found it a real struggle to get through the brambles and nettles into the wood proper. It was better once past that obstacle. The firs and spruce had been planted so close to each other that to make any headway standing up was difficult and made as much noise as some animal crashing through the wood. If Cala's passenger, Ghalib Malouf, was concealed somewhere in the wood, Gunn reckoned he would be warned of anyone's approach long before any attempt to prevent him taking a shot at the Prime Minister of Pakistan.

The branches from ground level up for seven or eight feet had died and fallen off, so Gunn was able to make reasonably stealthy progress without advertising his presence. On the ground there was a thick layer of pine and spruce needles which muffled any noise of his progress, but another problem Gunn quickly discovered was how easy it was to lose his sense of direction because of the darkness caused by the densely packed trees. He had removed his shooting jacket, hat and gaiters which he had left with his shot gun in the Landrover. He had taken the Glock 17 out of his jacket and pushed it into the pocket of his trousers. Time was not on his side as he made his way as fast as possible through the wood. In the distance he heard the sound of the Unimogs driving along the ride to drop off the guns. That sound also gave him a more accurate sense of direction, but he judged that he still had something like a hundred yards or more to go. The sound of the Unimogs diminished as they drove out of the ride in preparation for the beaters to start the drive. It was still about fifty yards to the ride where Gunn could just discern the light from the ride filtering through the trees.

The hunting horn sounded and was answered by the gamekeeper's whistle. Gunn scrambled through the trees favouring speed instead of silence. The PM and his High Commissioner would be in the centre of the drive on their 7 peg. Only about twenty yards now to the ride, but Gunn was not going to make it in time. He reached down and pulled the Glock out of his pocket in the hope that he still might be able to prevent Ghalib Malouf from shooting the PM. In the distance the sound of the beaters' calls and stick tapping reached Gunn and then came the first shots from the guns in the ride. Gunn cursed as it was now too late to prevent the assassination of the PM. He was now only a few yards from the ride and could just make out the pair on the number 7 peg. There was no sign of Malouf.

'Shit!' Gunn cursed under his breath. Had he got it all wrong? Was Malouf on the other side of the ride? The PM was having an excellent drive as the majority of birds were flying over the centre of the ride, which meant he could barely load his gun quick enough. Beside him, the High Commissioner looked distinctly uncomfortable and had moved clear of the PM, which indicated to Gunn that he was expecting something to happen. The beaters were now only a few yards away from the far side of the ride and the last of the birds which had been running ahead of them burst out of the undergrowth and soared across the ride. The dogs were busy picking up birds, many of which had fallen on Gunn's side of the ride and it was a black Labrador with a pheasant in its mouth which alerted Gunn to the bizarre spectacle which he had missed. The dog dropped the pheasant, its hackles rose and it snarled loudly at something behind Gunn. He dropped to the ground and swung round, the Glock automatic held in both hands. Only inches from where his head had been were the feet of a man's body hanging by the neck from the branch of a large spruce. On the ground below his feet was a shot gun.

'Ghalib Malouf, I presume,' Gunn muttered replacing the Glock back in his pocket. He dialled DCI Nesbit's number on his cellphone. It was answered immediately. 'I'm in the trees on the south side of the ride in Witches' Wood. I'm about ten yards in from the centre of the ride. I'm standing by the body of what I presume is Ghalib Malouf who arrived with Cala Williamson. He's hanging from a tree and is very dead. I'll wait for you here. I suggest we minimise the disruption to the Duke's shoot. All the guns are moving off now to the next drive. Neither Cala nor her father could have been anywhere near Malouf when he was killed so it would seem that there is another killer on the Estate.'

*

The shoot continued without further incident as the police cordoned off the crime scene while it was examined in minute detail. On completion of the final drive, the Chief Constable of Hampshire, Alex Marshall, accompanied by DCI Nesbit, met with the Prime Minister of Pakistan and the Duke of Cranborne. He was told of the alleged involvement of the High Commissioner in a conspiracy to supply nuclear warheads to the Taliban. Hassen Nassar, the High Commissioner, was spared the indignity of arrest because of his diplomatic status, but on the instructions of the Pakistan PM he was escorted onto a PIA flight back to Karachi that same night and was arrested on arrival at the airport in Pakistan. His daughter was arrested, but released on bail pending further investigation of any complicity in the conspiracy.

Gunn gave his statement to the police, bade farewell to the Cranborne dynasty, declined the offer of a brace of pheasants and drove back to London. The Chief Constable and the DCI had made it quite clear that the four murders connected with the shoot were now the prerogative of the Hampshire Police. Gunn contacted the BID Operations Centre and told the duty officer that he was signing off from his assignment, returning home and would be in the office on Monday to submit his report on the Granvil Estate shoot.

On Monday Gunn went to the office allocated to him for this latest assignment by David Simpson, the Head of Espionage. He had just set himself up with office laptop and had started typing his report when the phone rang.

'Gunn.'

'John, it's Angela. The boss would like you to come to his office asap. Heads of E and CE are here already.'

'On my way,' and Gunn put down the phone after the summons by the Director's PA. It was only one floor up to the Director's office and he reached it in a couple of minutes. Angela showed him into the office. Apart from the Director and his two Department Heads, the fourth person in the office was Wasem Halabi, the Pakistan Prime Minister.

'John, you've met His Excellency,' Miles Thompson did the introductions.

'Yes sir,' and Gunn shook hands with the PM.

'Please take a seat everyone and then the Prime Minister will explain the purpose of his visit.' When the five of them were seated in comfortable chairs, Wasem Halibi began.

'Director and gentlemen,' thank you for agreeing to meet me. Your Secretary of State believed that this was the right forum for me to explain our problem. Earlier this year you arrested three terrorists, one of whom was Irfan Nassar, a cousin of our ex-High Commissioner in London. They were alleged to be planning a bombing outrage in this Country. After their arrest, officers from my Country's Inter-Services Intelligence searched the properties where they had been staying in the North-West Tribal Area during their radical indoctrination and terrorist training. Some of the papers discovered in a cavity under the floor in one of the houses, all written in a code which took our ISI some time to decipher, concerned a conspiracy to provide the Taliban with a nuclear warhead together with the equipment and instructions to detonate it. At first our ISI believed that it had snuffed out this conspiracy before it had been activated because an audit of our nuclear weapons storage facilities at Kahuta and Khushab confirmed that all warheads were present and accounted for. Three days ago, while

I was on my way to your Country, I received a message from the ISI that Mohammed Ali Qureshi, the Controller of the nuclear storage facility, had been arrested and during his interrogation he admitted that he had falsified the audit check of the weapons under his control. Two 100 kiloton warheads are missing from the storage facility at Khushab.'

'Last night I spoke with Azil Zadari, our President. We are both aware that the influence of the Taliban warlords and Al Quaeda reaches into every corner of our Government, Public Service and Armed Forces.' Wasem Halabi paused and took a sip from the glass of water in front of him. 'I am here, of course, on his approval and recommendation and he told me to be as candid as possible about our security measures to safeguard our nuclear sites. Apart from warning the Western Governments via this meeting of the possibility that these nuclear weapons are in the hands of the Taliban, my President has authorised me to ask the British Intelligence Directorate for the services of one of its agents to come to Pakistan and help us trace those warheads. Your Prime Minister and Secretary of State have given their approval, but the final decision rests with you Sir Miles. If you agree to help us, then of course, who you send is your decision, but I was most impressed by Mr Gunn here,' and the PM turned towards Gunn, 'and although he does not speak Urdu, his Arabic is good. There you are gentlemen.' Wasem Halabi took another sip of water.

'The Prime Minister has been candid in his request to us,' Miles Thompson replied, 'so let's be equally candid and realistic with our response. Firstly, David; Gunn works for you and this operation would be driven by your Department.'

'We have a number of agents, Prime Minister, who can speak fluent Urdu,' David Simpson replied. 'I understand that you have met Mr Gunn and your wish that he should be our selection to assist you if our Director approves the request. Please allow us to make the selection of agent.'

'Michael, your views,' the Director asked.

'The selection of agent must be David's prerogative,' Michael Carrington agreed.

'Prime Minister,' Miles began, 'I understand that you will be in London for a further 48 hours. I assure you we will identify an agent to come to Pakistan, but who that agent is must be my decision.'

'Thank you, Miles,' and Wasem Halabi said his farewells and was escorted from the BID building.

*

Gunn returned to his office and completed his report. The phone rang as he was reading through it.

'Gunn.'

'David Simpson John; after some discussion with Miles, I've decided to task Richard Lamb with this assignment. I'm sorry if that's a disappointment for you, but you will know that his background is eminently suitable to the location and circumstances of this request by the Prime Minister of Pakistan.'

'No problem, sir; it will give me a chance to catch up with my paperwork. Thank you for letting me know.'

Gunn had known David Simpson ever since he was a controller in the Middle East Section of BID's Espionage Department. David had been promoted to Director of the Department after the previous Director had been murdered in his office by his PA who, it transpired, was a 'sleeper' for the Russian Federal Security Service. Gunn's paperwork consisted of contacting Malcolm Springfield, ex-RAF Squadron Leader and BID's senior helicopter pilot, to arrange an hour's session in the Directorate's new Lynx helicopter which had replaced the Gazelle. That was followed by a visit to the building's basement where he had his usual competition with BID's Armourer, ex-Small Arms School instructor, Tony Taylor. It was on his way back from the basement of Kingsroad House that events took a different turn. He was heading back to his office to make arrangements to spend a week of self-inflicted torture at BID's training centre in Maidenhead where the instructors—most of them ex-Army Physical Training Corps—would pound his muscles and ligaments daily until they considered that he was properly fit for duty. His cellphone rang; it was the Director's PA summoning him to the boss's office again. He took the lift to the 14th floor. David Simpson was with the Director when he was shown into the office.

'John, there's been a change of plan,' Miles Thompson began. 'On the news tonight and in the papers tomorrow you will read of the death of Richard Lamb. He was discovered by his cleaner around ten this morning. Cause of death not yet confirmed, but it wasn't the cause that was so bizarre it was how he was found. His body was found in an empty bath zipped up in a sports bag. Both the police and Counter Espionage are involved in the investigation, but that of course meant that David had to find a replacement to go to Pakistan. All the E Department Urdu speakers are already tasked so it looks as though the Pakistan Prime Minister will get his choice of agent. Problems?'

'None, sir.'

'Your briefing sequence will start at nine tomorrow morning. You might want to go back to your house in Chelsea to sort out anything that needs sorting.'

*

As far as Gunn was concerned, the main thing that needed sorting was his lack of knowledge of Pakistan. On his way back to his small mews house in Elm Park Lane, Gunn called in at WH Smiths in the Brompton Road and picked up a paperback copy of the 'Rough Guide' which he read from cover to cover that evening. The next morning he reported to the section which covered the Indian Sub-Continent and Pakistan. The Assistant Director of the section was Richard Preston and his controller, Stephanie Travis, were both in the office when he was shown in by the AD's PA, Poppy. The third person in the office was introduced as Martin Whistler, Head of International Sales for Universal Switchgear plc.

'Mr Whistler's company does a considerable amount of business in Pakistan,' Richard Preston began once the introductions were completed. 'His company produces every type of electronic switching equipment for every aspect of manufacturing industry including that associated with nuclear power plants and satellites. After your briefing here today you will be spending three days at Universal Switchgear's engineering works in Milton Keynes. You will be going to Islamabad as a marketing consultant working for Universal Switchgear. I won't keep you any longer Mr Whistler. Mr Gunn will be staying at the Plaza Hotel.'

After Martin Whistler had left the office escorted from the building by one of the BID security guards, Gunn's briefing followed the usual format covering Pakistan's history of confrontation with India which had been the spur for its acquisition of nuclear weapons, its political background and as much as was known about the quantity and location of all Pakistan's nuclear facilities. Gunn was given the contact details of Javed Iqbal, BID's in-country agent; he, like all other British Embassies and High Commissions had replaced the MI6 officers who had been removed during the 1988 reorganisation of the UK's intelligence organisation. Javed lived in Islamabad and his existence was only known to the British High Commissioner, his deputy and the Defence Attaché.

'May I know how Universal Switchgear was identified as my cover while I'm in Pakistan?' Gunn interrupted the rather glib briefing delivery. His interruption was not expected and evidently irritated Richard Preston, the AD of the Indian sub-continent section. Stephanie Travis, his controller for the assignment, looked uncomfortable.

'The recommendation came from Alan Thomas, the High Commissioner. Why do you ask?'

'That's very simple sir; four people have been killed in the last week in connection with this assignment—maybe even five, if poor Richard's bizarre death is included. The police, with the best will in the world, haven't a clue other than the obvious arrest and release of Cala Williamson and the expulsion of her father from this Country. They are still looking for the killer of Ghalib Malouf. I've no doubt that Universal Switchgear is a highly reputable company, but I want to know who is in the 'loop' of these missing warheads.

The High Commission has a large Defence Section, no less than five officers and one senior rank when I checked with Google last night. As yet this briefing has included nothing about the military personnel in the High Commission. I may be jumping the gun, but how much do they know, is that relevant and if it is, is that included in this brief?'

'Yes, of course,' the AD confirmed, but the remainder of the briefing failed to allay Gunn's cynicism about the AD's casual approach to this assignment.

After the AD's briefing, Gunn did the usual rounds of the Operations Centre, Codes and Ciphers, Medical Centre and Armoury where Tony Taylor checked his two Glocks and then told him that he would be met at the airport by Javed Iqbal who would provide him with new Glocks and a very sensitive Geiger-counter. His last call was to Malcolm Springfield where he was put through a thorough workout in the Lynx for two hours. As soon as that was over, Gunn returned to his mews house in Chelsea, packed an overnight bag and caught the train from Euston Station to Milton Keynes.

On arrival at the hotel Gunn was told that his room was Number 211. He asked if the hotel was full and when told that it was not asked if he might change his room.

'On that floor, sir, both 215 and 217 are available for three nights,' the receptionist told him.

'217 will do nicely, thank you.' The receptionist handed him a message informing him that he would be met at 8.30 the next morning by Ms Emma Pankhurst, Universal Switchgear's Head of Marketing.

CHAPTER 9

'I thought the recommendation to use Universal Switchgear as Gunn's cover came from David Crawford-Slade, the Commercial Councillor at the High Commission,' Stephanie queried after Gunn had left the office.

'Yes it did, but any advice from a High Commission has to be cleared by the Head of Mission,' the AD replied as he collected up his briefing papers and returned them to the folder on his desk.

'I know he was cleared of any involvement by the investigation, but wasn't it Crawford-Slade who the Pakistani ISI wanted to interview about that drug scandal earlier this year which came too close for comfort to the High Commission?' Stephanie persisted.

'Yes, I believe it was,' Preston confirmed dismissively. 'I expect you'll want to get on with Gunn's flight details.' On that note, Stephanie realised that any further comment was wasted, so she picked up her copy of the briefing papers and left the AD's office.

'I wonder,' she muttered as she returned to her office.

As the door closed behind Stephanie, the AD stopped making a performance of tidying the briefing papers on his desk and looked up at the closed door.

'Shit!' he cursed aloud as he followed Stephanie out of his office. He stuck his head round the door of his PA's office. 'I'll be out of the office for twenty minutes. I've forgotten to get a card for my mother's birthday.' He left the building and headed for the three telephone boxes on the corner of Cale Street and Sydney Street where he made his call.

The CCTV camera mounted on the side of the Royal Brompton Hospital recorded his visit to the telephone boxes and relayed the digital video back to BID's Operation Centre.

*

Gunn had finished his breakfast by 8.15 the next morning and walked out to the lobby of the hotel to watch the comings and goings of hotel life in Milton Keynes. His cellphone rang.

'Yes,' he wasn't familiar with the number shown on the phone.

'Steph from the office; do you know if you'll be in the hotel this evening?'

'No idea Steph, I'm waiting in the hotel lobby for my guide from Universal Switchgear. Once I've met her I should have an idea what programme has been arranged. Why? Is there a problem?'

'Yes, I believe so, but would rather speak with you on neutral ground.'

'Understood, I'll call you back as soon as I know the programme....'

'John Gunn?' the query interrupted his call from Stephanie.

'Hang on Steph, my guide's arrived; call you back asap,' and Gunn disconnected the call from his controller. 'Yes, that is I and you must be Emma Pankhurst.'

'Wow, what grammar! Call from your wife?'

'No, from the office, Emma: is anything planned for this evening?'

'That's up to you John. I've been told that I'm at your service for these three days.'

'What time will we be back here this evening?'

'Shortly after seven.'

'Thanks, I'll just send this text and then no more interruptions.' Gunn sent a text to Stephanie telling her that He hoped to be free by 7pm and then turned to Emma. 'Right Emma, now I'm ready to learn all about switchgear and I bet your good looks market lots of it.'

'That's very gallant of you, John. Is that part of the Diplomatic Service package?'

'I shouldn't think so for a moment,' Gunn replied as a black Mercedes C class Saloon drove in under the portico of the Plaza Hotel and a uniformed driver got out and opened the rear door. Gunn's comment about her looks was well-deserved; a figure-hugging business suit, genuine tan and jet black hair had turned most of the male heads in the lobby. She got in the car first followed by Gunn. 'But then I don't work for the Diplomatic Service if that is what you've been told,' he added as the door was shut.

'The memo I received from Martin said that I would be escorting a John Gunn from the Foreign and Commonwealth Office.'

'No, I work for the Intelligence Directorate.' Ever since the start of the assignment had interrupted his holiday in Monaco, everything about it had seemed to Gunn like the topsy-turvy world of Alice in Wonderland where nothing was what it first appeared to be; like walking through a hall of distorting mirrors at a fun fair. Why had the AD opted for Richard Lamb when the Pakistan PM had asked for him? The AD had made out that it was his lack of Urdu, but Lamb had only started learning Urdu recently and his Arabic was non-existent. Who had killed Lamb in such weird circumstances? Why was the AD's briefing so inept? Gunn reckoned that he'd learned more about Pakistan from the 'Rough Guide'. Who was the killer—still at large—on the Granvil Estate and why did Steph want to come and speak with him on 'neutral ground'? All of these questions required answers so Gunn was determined to force the pace of this assignment by making it plain who he was, if for no other reason, to see if it made anyone 'break cover'. It had partially worked down in Lower Shalford when he'd announced in the pub that he worked for BID which had resulted in Alec Moore's attempt to kill him by sabotaging his shotgun, so why not try again? Even on the thick carpeting in the Mercedes, the proverbial drop of a pin might have been heard. The driver had certainly heard so that, Gunn hoped, would be rapidly spread around the employees of Universal Switchgear.

'So you're a sort of secret agent?' Emma broke the silence which had followed Gunn's explanation of which Government department he worked for.

'Hopefully, a little more professional than 'sort of'', but yes, that's what I do for a living.'

The Mercedes stopped at a steel gate which opened automatically to allow the car to drive forward to a barrier. A uniformed security guard came out of a kiosk, checked the driver's ID and then his guide's ID. After that he came round to the other side of the car.

'Do you have any ID, sir, so that I can check your name off the list of today's visitors.' Gunn's window had been lowered by the driver so he showed his BID ID to the security guard. The guard pressed a button on a remote device and the barrier lifted.

'So far so good,' Gunn thought. The Mercedes drove on through a series of modern, clean buildings to a central larger building fronted by a car park. 'Universal appears to take its security seriously,' he muttered.

'Sorry, what was that?' his guide asked.

'Impressive security, Emma, has there ever been a break-in to this complex?'

'Not in the four years that I have worked for Universal. Harry, please stop by the steps. I'll call the motor pool if I'm going to need you again.'

'Yes, that's fine Miss Pankhurst.' Once again the door was opened and Gunn got out followed by Emma. He followed her up the wide flight of shallow steps enjoying the sight of her backside in the tight skirt, but then stopped. Emma paused and turned.

'Anything wrong John?'

'On the contrary, it's all perfectly right,' he joked which made her smile, but he'd seen something in the row of cars parked facing the building which added to the 'Wonderland' puzzle; a black Range Rover with a personal registration plate PUR 66. The last time he'd seen that car was on the Granvil Estate and the plate belonged to Richard Jardine, Marquess of Purbeck.

*

The first port of call was Emma's office in the marketing department on the third floor of the building which appeared to be constructed of 90% glass—the remaining 10% was steel and concrete. In her office, Emma quickly explained the programme for the three days of his initiation into the machinations of Universal Switchgear. Once that was over his tour of the site and buildings began in earnest. Emma drove him from one building to another in an electric golf buggy. It was while she was driving the buggy that she told him that he would be meeting the Managing Director of the Company, Sir Norman Stonehouse, at an informal finger-buffet lunch which was being held in the boardroom suite of rooms in the main building. During the morning, Gunn had been shown that the Company produced almost every conceivable electric device from the humble household electric light switch through steering wheel gear-change paddles on Formula 1 racing cars to detonating devices for fusion nuclear weapons. The tour was fascinating, but throughout it, Gunn kept seeing the Range Rover and wondering what on earth Richard Jardine was doing at Universal Switchgear. He decided that was the first question he intended to put to the MD at the 'informal lunch'.

Promptly at 12.30, Emma delivered him to the seventh floor of the main building where visitors were already gathering for lunch in the Company's entertainment suite of rooms. Gunn recognised many of Universal's employees whom he had met that morning. He accepted a flute of chilled champagne from a waitress in a little black dress which seemed a couple of sizes too small for her, or perhaps Gunn reflected, she was purposely a couple of sizes too ample for the the dress. Emma spotted Gunn's appreciation of the girl's mobile backside as she moved among the guests with her salver of champagne-filled flutes.

'Now, now John, business before pleasure, come and meet the MD.'

'Nice ass, as our American cousins would say,' Gunn commented and obediently followed Emma's equally 'nice ass' through the now crowded room in the direction of the Managing Director. Nearly there, she stopped and turned to Gunn.

'Is it OK to introduce you as a BID officer?'

'Yes fine, I'd be grateful if you would do that.'

Confidently and politely, Emma caught her boss's eye who had been talking to another guest at the lunch.

'Sir Norman, I would like you to meet Mr Gunn from the British Intelligence Directorate who is a guest of the Company for the next three days.'

'Thank you Emma,' the MD acknowledged. 'You are shortly going to Pakistan, Mr Gunn, I believe. We have a considerable number of contracts in that Country. How was this morning and do you have any questions for me?'

'Yes sir, a slightly odd one from 'left field'.'

'Go on Mr Gunn, that'll make an interesting change,' the older man said. Gunn was aware of the MD's steady gaze concentrated on him.

'Last weekend I was at a shoot on the Duke of Cranborne's Estate. The police were investigating a murder of one of our officers from BID and I was there to assist with security for the senior diplomatic guests. I shall be going to Pakistan shortly at the request of the Prime Minister, Wasem Halabi, to assist in further enquiries connected with their nuclear weapons programme which is why I'm here. When I arrived here this morning, I noticed that there was a black Range Rover in your car park outside this building which belongs to the Duke's elder son, Lord Purbeck. I was wondering why Lord Purbeck is visiting Universal Switchgear?' and to himself 'now let's see if I get a straight answer to that question.'

'Yes, of course, Miles Thompson spoke to me a couple of days ago to set up your visit and mentioned the loss of two of your officers. Lord Purbeck's visit? . . . . I believe that was arranged with

Martin Whistler, my Head of International Sales,' the MD replied looking enquiringly at Emma.

'Yes sir, that is what I understood,' she confirmed.

'What would be Lord Purbeck's interest in Pakistan sir?' Gunn persisted.

'As I understand it from my Sales Director, Lord Purbeck has many contacts in the Country which date back to the time of the Raj. Both the Indians and Pakistanis set great store by these historical alliances and I expect that Lord Purbeck felt that he could be of help as a consultant to our sales division.'

'But he was not invited to lunch.'

'You are persistent with your questioning Mr Gunn.'

'That's my job sir.'

'Quite right; I will have an answer to that question before you leave today. Now, Mr Gunn, tell me what you can about your job and what we can do to help you prepare for your visit to Pakistan.'

'If you can spare the time sir, I would welcome the opportunity of doing that in your office, but not here,' Gunn replied

'Of course . . . . Emma, please speak to Rhoda and ask her to find a slot this afternoon when Mr Gunn and I can have twenty minutes undisturbed conversation in my office. Now Mr Gunn I will leave you in the capable hands of Emma while I do my duty to today's guests,' and with that arrangement made the MD of Universal Switchgear moved off among his guests. Gunn had noticed that the flute in his hand held only water.

'You've clearly stirred his interest, John. Our Sir Norman is something of a recluse apart from being a Nobel Prize winner for his work in physics . . . . I think it was astro-physics. He usually gets the Deputy MD to host visitors like you.'

'Who is your Deputy MD?' Gunn asked.

'That's Doctor Helen McPhearson; she's away at the moment in the States, but is back tomorrow and I will take you to meet her. Right, shall we continue with our programme?'

'Lead on, Emma,' and the two of them left the buffet lunch. There was no sign of the black Range Rover when they came out of the building.

The MD's PA, Rhoda, contacted Gunn and Emma half-an-hour later while they were in a 'clean' area, dressed in white overalls and 'shower caps' examining the circuitry for a British communication satellite. They shed their overalls and caps and returned to the main building. Gunn then spent exactly twenty minutes explaining the background to the assignment to the MD and the reason why he had revealed that he worked for the British Intelligence Directorate.

After the meeting with Sir Norman Stonehouse, Gunn collected Emma from the PA's office where he was told that the next department to be visited was the largest building on the Company's industrial estate where huge reels of armoured, submarine communication cables were manufactured and exported all over the world. They were escorted out of the Company's Head Office building by a security guard before re-joining their electric buggy for the ride to the far end of the industrial estate and its largest warehouse. Throughout his tour, Gunn had been aware of the presence of security guards, certainly guarding access to the estate, but also in all the buildings which they had visited. This level of security had impressed him, but this was the first time that their buggy appeared to have developed a 'tail'. Gunn had first spotted it as they turned a corner, otherwise, as the rear-view mirror was angled for the buggy driver, it would have gone unnoticed.

'Emma, it may be my imagination, but are we being escorted or followed by that buggy which has tailed us ever since leaving your Head Office building?' Gunn asked having noticed that Emma was also keeping an eye on it in the rear-view mirror.

'You've seen it too, John. That's neither Company policy nor practice. I'm responsible for your security, not the security guards.'

For the first time since their meeting at the hotel that morning, Gunn noticed that his guide looked both anxious and uncertain on what course of action to take.

'OK, here's what we do, Emma. Bear in mind that four people have already been murdered to prevent BID from discovering what connects the Granvil Estate in Hampshire with Pakistan and now, apparently, Universal Switchgear. There is no need for you to become involved, so when we get to the cable warehouse, where you told me we would be met by the manager of that department, you stay with the buggy . . . .'

'. . . . no way!' Emma interrupted. 'I was given the job of looking after you and that's what I intend to do. I'll be fucking angry if there are some rotten apples in our barrel involved in some form of conspiracy. And what's more, John Gunn, I'm not a weak little female . . . . I'll have you know I've a brown belt in Karate and I'm captain of the Company's ladies' football team . . . . here we are,' Emma interrupted herself. 'That's Harvey Greenwood, the Manager of the cable division, standing in front of those large open doors. Oh!' she added, glancing in the rear-view mirror, 'the buggy following us has turned off towards another building . . . . perhaps a false alarm . . . . are you armed?' Emma concluded, stopping the buggy by the huge hangar-like doors of the cable building.

'Yes,' was Gunn's one word reply.

'Cool! I wish I wasn't wearing these high-heeled shoes. They're useless if we're caught up in a chase . . . . just like *'Homeland'*, that TV CIA spy thriller,' she added getting nimbly out of the buggy. Gunn followed her and was introduced to Harvey Greenwood.

CHAPTER 10

The cable warehouse was huge. To Gunn it looked more like an aircraft hangar than a factory producing submarine communication cables. After the introduction Gunn discovered the true scale of the building when he was told that it was was 200 yards long, 40 yards wide and 50 feet high. At various stages along the inside of the warehouse were manufacturing stations producing the eight layers of waterproofing and protection for the fibre-optic core which would carry the thousands of simultaneous communications. But for the presence of the security guard who had followed them from the Head Office, Gunn would have enjoyed taking an intelligent interest in the tour round the cable warehouse instead of concentrating on anything and everything that might threaten the three of them.

Emma and Gunn had been issued with white hard-hats and overalls before the start of the tour. Everyone else working in the warehouse was wearing dark blue overalls and yellow hard-hats, so their small group of three was purposely—for safety reasons—easily identifiable. Above their heads were powerful gantry cranes which carried the twenty ton drums of completed cable to the serried ranks of forty-ton flat-bed trucks at the far end of the building and from there, Harvey Greenwood told them, they were transported to special cable-laying ships all over the world. Gunn noticed that the current drum moving slowly above them was stamped with the tri-colour of the French Flag, *Câble de télécommunications* and the name of the cable-laying ship *FS Edith Piaff*.

The manager led them to the first station in the warehouse where the fibre-optic core began its journey along the production line which ran the length of the building. At successive stations the Manager told them that the core was wrapped in petroleum jelly, copper sheathing, polycarbonate, aluminium, steel binding, Mylar and finally a polythene outer layer before it was coiled onto a huge drum and lifted by the gantry crane.

A flash of reflected light and movement above the drum distracted Gunn, who unceremoniously pushed both Emma and the Manager clear of the area under the drum of submarine cable.

C R A S H!!! . . . . there was a deafening thunder of noise as a twenty ton drum of cable crashed onto the hardened concrete floor of the warehouse, exactly where the three of them had been standing barely seconds before. Splinters of the disintegrating wooden casing of the drum flew everywhere like missiles injuring many of the men and women working in the vicinity. The freed cable erupted out of the shattered drum uncoiling, weaving and squirming like some vast prehistoric serpent, knocking people over, breaking bones and smashing equipment.

'John!' Emma shouted at the top of her voice. She had lost sight of him in the chaos and hubbub of the alarm siren and First Aiders rushing to help the injured employees. There was no sign of Gunn and Emma had to be restrained by the Manager from rushing into the maelstrom of rescuers and First Aiders to search for him amongst the cable drum wreckage. An instant after the drum crashed to the warehouse floor, the Manager had triggered an alarm with a remote device he had been carrying. He then used his cellphone to dial treble nine. Para-medics from the Company's 'in-house' medical staff were on the scene in minutes, closely followed by ambulances from Milton Keynes Hospital.

The foreman of the fibre-optic station had been explaining the construction of a submarine cable just moments before the cable drum crashed to the floor of the warehouse. Gunn had been momentarily distracted from the explanation by a reflection of light from high up in the roof area where catwalks criss-crossed the eaves of the warehouse to provide maintenance access to the gantry cranes. Quickly checking that both Emma and the Manager had recovered from being roughly pushed clear of the area where they had been standing under the craned drum, Gunn had slipped away, discarded his white overalls and hard hat and climbed up a steel staircase at the side of the building which led in two stages to the catwalks in the roof area.

'There it is again!' Gunn said aloud as he started up the second stage of the staircase. Something was reflecting light from the powerful arc lamps which lit the interior of the warehouse. Below him the noise of ambulance sirens and the rescue and treatment of the injured carried clearly up into the roof area. He heard Emma shout his name. For a moment he stopped and lost his footing on the narrow staircase. That might well have saved his life as the bullet aimed at his head ricocheted off the steel handrail and whined up into the roof to bury itself in the insulating material below the roof canopy.

The security guard was sitting astride the gantry crane which had released the cable drum. The large 'I' beam on which the crane lifting mechanism was mounted stretched the full width of the warehouse. It was moving slowly along the rails on either side of the warehouse towards one of the catwalks. Gunn assumed that the 'I' beam's progress could be stopped at the point where it passed underneath a catwalk so that maintenance work could be carried out on the powerful electric motor and upper and lower sheaves of the crane.

Below the crane, relative calm had returned. The alarm siren had been switched off and the process of removing the injured employees out to the ambulances was almost finished. The Manager and any number of other people had now seen the drama developing in the catwalk area of the roof above them. The Manager moved quickly to the side of the warehouse where, at each manufacturing station, there was a bank of circuit breakers which could stop the production line and cranes in the event of just such an emergency. He closed off the main breaker and both the crane and the production line came to a halt.

The 'I' beam with the crane mechanism and security guard had stopped about five feet away from the servicing catwalk. At this stage, Gunn had not even taken the Glock 17 out of the holster in the small of his back and was extremely reluctant to shoot at the guard whom he hoped to interrogate to establish the connection between Universal Switchgear and the Granvil Estate—if any. The guard fired another shot at Gunn before he climbed onto the 'I' beam, either with the intention of leaping onto the catwalk or to walk along the beam to the other side of the warehouse. Gunn reckoned that both options posed considerable risks.

Down below the guard on the warehouse production line, the Manager had also seen what was about to happen. Hanging down from the crane on a cable connected to the crane mechanism was a remote control box. The Manager reached up and pulled the remote control box down, operated one of the switches and then nodded to the station foreman who pushed up the circuit breaker. The 'I' beam began to move again, but in reverse, away from the catwalk. Desperately the security guard tried to regain his balance on the 'I' beam as it moved away from the catwalk and then leapt across the ever-widening gap between the beam and the catwalk. He managed to get a handhold on the guardrail of the catwalk with his left hand, but was still holding the automatic in his right hand. The automatic fell from his grasp and clattered down onto the warehouse floor forty feet below. His whole weight was now held by his left hand as he desperately tried to reach up with his right hand to grab the guardrail. Seeing that the guard was unarmed, the Manager reversed the beam back towards the catwalk. Gunn raced up the last flight of stairs and jumped onto the catwalk. The beam was still moving and in a few seconds would be under the flailing feet of the security guard. As Gunn lay on the catwalk and reached down to grab the man's wrist, his hand slipped off the guardrail and, screaming, he fell the forty feet to the concrete floor below.

'Shit!' Gunn cursed; 'so much for my chance of getting some information out of him.' He stood up, went down the metal staircase and joined the group of people clustered around the body as it was transferred into the back of an ambulance.

'Are you OK?' Emma asked.

'Yes, I'm fine thanks; who's the man and did he say anything before they started to load him into the ambulance.'

Emma turned to the Manager who had taken control of the hiatus and repeated the question which Gunn had asked. The latter shook his head and turned to the senior paramedic as the ambulance doors shut. The vehicle moved away from the hangar doors of the Submarine Communication Cable Division of Universal Switchgear.

'He was dead by the time he entered the ambulance, but my colleague here,' and he pointed to his fellow paramedic, 'said that he was muttering about 'witches' or something that sounded like that . . . . could have been 'midges', he interrupted himself as his colleague gave him more information.

'I don't suppose that's of any value Mr Gunn,' the Manager said, turning to Gunn.

'Thank you . . . . a possibility, but little more than that. Who was this security guard? Has anyone got a name for him?' Gunn asked with a fairly high note of incredulity in his query. Gunn's query caused a considerable amount of embarrassment, particularly to the 'on site' Head of the security firm, Guardian Shield, which provided Universal's physical security. He, like the man just removed, was in uniform. Having spotted the man, Gunn repeated the question. 'He's one of yours, so what's his name?' It was as Gunn asked the question that he realised what it was that had alerted him to the presence of the rogue guard up in the roof catwalk. On the man's right breast pocket was a large and shiny copper shield with the security firm's logo on it. The powerful light from the roof arc lamps had reflected off this shield.

'Are you in charge here?' the Head of the security firm asked lamely.

'No, Mr Greenwood is the manager in charge.'

'May I speak to you in private, sir?' the man asked addressing his question to the Manager of the Division.

'In due course, yes, but you've been asked to identify the guard who shot at our visitor so please do so without any further delay.'

'I have no idea who he is . . . . was. I have never seen him since we started our contract here four years ago.'

'Well that opens a real can of worms which will have to be dealt with as a separate issue. Emma, I suggest you take Mr Gunn back to his hotel and we can reconvene his visit to my Division first thing tomorrow morning. My apologies Mr Gunn, we don't usually have this level of excitement during a visit,' and with that apology from the Manager, the visit finished and Gunn returned to the Plaza Hotel with Emma.

On the journey back in the car Emma was silent until they were almost at the hotel. 'I saw the gun in that holster on your belt, but you never drew it even though that guard was shooting at you. Was that because you wanted to question the man?' Emma asked.

'In a word, yes; your company, or perhaps I should focus my criticism on Guardian Shield, has been extremely incompetent to let that man into your restricted area. I need to know how he did that. Fortunately he was a rotten shot which makes me think that he was unused to firing an automatic. So is there somewhere I can get away from hotel food and if there is would you be able to join me for some supper?'

'Yes, lots of places ranging from bloody awful greasy spoons to restaurants which genuinely qualify for their five stars. The Company will pay—that text has just come through from Rhoda, Sir Norman's PA. Apparently he's furious about the incident at the Cable Division. He's insisted on an immediate inquiry to find out who the rogue guard was and how he got past security. He has directed that the report will be on his desk by 8.30 tomorrow morning so that he can show it to you. So, pick you up in a company car at 7.30?' she ended on a questioning note.

'Look forward to it,' and Gunn got out of the car and went into the hotel. He paused at Reception and glanced at the numbered slots for each room behind the receptionist. Both his room 217 and the next door one, 215 were empty. The new shift had replaced the one which had booked him in to the hotel and probably had no idea who he was. 'Have there been any messages for 215?' One of the duty receptionists glanced at the 215 slot and then at the computer VDU in front of her and shook her head assuming that he was the occupant booked into room 215.

'No Mr Campbell.'

Gunn turned away to head for the lifts, but was called back by the Day Manager.

'One moment Mr Campbell; there were no messages, but we had to do some minor electrical repairs to several rooms on the second floor including yours and 217 and 213 on either side. Nothing's been disturbed sir.'

'Thank you,' Gunn acknowledged and turned away from the lifts and headed for the stairs. 'Too many fucking unexplained 'coincidences',' he muttered as he started up the stairs.

The second floor lobby was deserted as was the corridor in both directions except for the cleaning trolley which was parked outside one of the rooms. The trolley was outside room 212 on the other side of the corridor. There was no sign of the trolley's owner. Gunn pushed it across the corridor to his room, inserted his plastic key card into the slot and withdrew it. The green light lit; he gave the door a hard shove and crouching down behind the trolley, pushed it into the room.

There were two men in the room, both wearing ski masks over their heads; one was armed with a baseball bat and the other with a steel crowbar. The sharp edge of the trolley hit the crowbar man who was closer to Gunn in the crutch and disabled him for long enough for Gunn to deal with the other man. Once he had removed the baseball bat, he blocked the man's flailing and inaccurate punches with clinical chops and blows which left him semi-conscious on the carpet. The man whose groin had taken the full force of the trolley showed signs of recovering so Gunn used the baseball bat to put him out of action. He pulled off the masks and used curtain-ties to bind both men's hands and feet before phoning the manager. The latter arrived breathless and desperately anxious to avoid any adverse publicity for the hotel.

'Are these your electricians by any chance?' Gunn asked the manager showing him his BID ID.

'Yes . . . I believe they are . . . . this is 217, I thought you were Mr Campbell from 215, sir . . . .' the manager stammered on.

'Are you going to phone the police or shall I.'

'No . . . . of course I'll do that. I'm not sure of the number . . . .'

'Try 999, it usually works,' Gunn offered.

'Yes of course,' and the manager made the call with many 'ums and ahs', but the police emergency call centre eventually got the information it needed.

'May I suggest that you give your General Manager a call as I suspect that he might want to be around when the police get here,' Gunn offered. While he was waiting for the police, Gunn phoned Steph, told her what had occurred and asked her to speak to Scotland Yard. He also told her that he would arrange a meeting with her for the following day.

It was just short of twenty minutes when the police arrived in two cars. An inspector was the first into the hotel room. 'Is there a Mr Gunn here?'

'Yes Inspector, I'm Gunn,' he confirmed, showing his BID ID and grateful for Steph's alacrity in getting in touch with Scotland Yard.

'Inspector Ross, Thames Valley Police, Wolverton,' and showed Gunn his Police Warrant card. The Inspector glanced at the two men who had attacked Gunn.

'Oh, for god's sake, not these two again; the larger and uglier one is Marvin Winstone and the skinny one is Jacob Parker,' and he turned to the second policeman who had entered the hotel room. 'Sergeant Mills, get McBain and Clifford to give you a hand with these two.' Two other policemen came into the room and once the curtain ties had been removed from the men's ankles, they were properly handcuffed, arrested, cautioned and led out of the room. He then turned to the General Manager who had replaced his Day Manager.

'If you would like to go down to your office, sir, I will speak with Mr Gunn and we will then leave your hotel.' As soon as the General Manager had left the room the Inspector turned to Gunn. 'Your office called the Yard who briefed me on the drive over here. These two men can be hired by anyone and both have spent more of their lives locked up than out on the streets. If previous incidents like this are anything to go by, it will be impossible to discover who hired them as they don't know that themselves. Money would have changed hands in any one of the seedier pubs in Milton Keynes or Northampton. There's usually a third one—Ruben Freeman—who hangs around with these two, but he was dead-on-arrival at the hospital only a couple of hours ago. We've also arrested Mr Saddler, the duty manager of Guardian Shield, Universal Switchgear's security company, who has got some explaining to do. Can we have a statement from you, sir?'

'Of course,' and Gunn glanced at his watch—5.30—there was plenty of time before his supper date with Emma. 'I'll do that right now on hotel writing paper and you can take it with you.'

'Much appreciated, sir; Sergeant Mills will take the statement.'

It was nearly 7pm by the time the statement was signed and witnessed by Sgt Mills, but that gave Gunn just enough time for a shower before he was due to be picked up by Emma.

*

'How in god's name could you have made such a fuck-up of the simple task of getting rid of one man?'

'I tell you he leads a charmed life. Either that or he's considerably more skilful than you chose to tell me.'

'That's nonsense and you know it. When we set up Operation Breakback we all knew that there would need to be some wet action. That time has come and you've screwed it up. It's now become front page news instead of a small paragraph on the fifth page reporting a tragic shooting accident.'

'Alright, alright so what's the next move?'

'Can you complete the job tonight?'

'I can try.'

'Trying's not good enough. For fuck's sake get on with it and kill the fucking man!' and after that flow of expletives the phone was slammed down. The other phone was put down more slowly.

'Bye, bye John Gunn.'

CHAPTER 11

'Don't tell me you're in trouble again,' Emma teased as she met up with Gunn in the bar of the Plaza Hotel. 'It's chaos out there in reception with everyone talking about an assault on one of the guests and police removing a couple of thugs in handcuffs.' The bar was moderately full of people who had been attending a conference and other itinerant men and women over-nighting on business trips or one-night stands. Emma's arrival in the bar in her 'little-black-dress' which perfectly set off her figure had caused a momentary lull in the buzz of bar conversation. Gunn finished his whisky and water.

'Guilty as charged, your honour. Come on, I'll tell you all about it in the car, unless you'd like a drink here?'

'I can't let you out of my sight can I; no I can wait until we get to the restaurant and anyway I want to know what happened here.'

She took Gunn's arm as the two of them left the hotel. The company car was parked under the hotel's portico. Once they were both seated and on their way, Emma turned to Gunn.

'Right John, now tell me what happened as I shall have to relay this to Sir Norman. Incidentally, our driver tonight is Gary,'—the driver responded to this with a raised hand—he's Sir Norman's personal driver, but he told me that after today's events he wasn't prepared to entrust us to anyone else.' Gunn acknowledged the introduction and then gave Emma, and the driver, a very brief summary of the events after he arrived back at the hotel that afternoon. When he finished there was silence.

'How many times have these people tried to kill you?' Emma finally asked as their Mercedes C Class saloon headed north along the A5 towards Northampton.

'Four at the last count, but that's to be expected because I purposely announced my identity so that it would make these people do just that. Unfortunately I have only succeeded in digging the hired hands out of the woodwork so far, but shortly I'm hoping that will lead to the 'big cheeses'. Now, Emma, where are we going this evening?'

'The 'Happy Sole'—not much further; it's on a turn-off to the right from the A5. As you might guess it specialises in fish and seafood, but the menu covers a whole variety of other dishes.'

'Sounds good, now both of you listen to me. Whoever is trying to kill me and for whatever reason, it's more than likely that injury to those with me are dismissed as acceptable collateral damage . . . .'

'I know what you're . . . .' Emma started to interrupt.

'. . . . no please, just hear me out and then make your decision,' Gunn continued. 'In Lower Shalford, my predecessor had his head blown off because he had overheard a conversation between two Pakistani diplomats. For the same mistake, an innocent beater on the shoot who happened to understand Urdu was poisoned with a particularly painful and lethal substance known as Tetrodotoxin. The landlord of the pub where I was staying was very nearly killed by a booby-trapped shotgun meant for me and another man died who was trying to administer that same poison to me. A BID agent who should have been on this assignment that I'm now on was found dead in his flat, squashed into a sports bag. Both Emma and the manager of the cable division only just escaped being killed today by that drum and most recently we have the incident at the Plaza Hotel. Now guys, the government pays me to take these risks, whether I think I get paid enough is neither here nor there. Neither of you are paid to do that. Gary, are you married?'

'No sir, single. My wife was killed by a drunken driver two years ago. We had no children.'

'When we get to the restaurant,' Gunn continued, 'I would like you to take the Mercedes back to wherever it's kept. Emma and I will get a taxi back to the hotel.'

'Sorry sir, thanks for the offer, but I can't do that . . . . even if I wanted to. Sir Norman has given me strict instructions about looking after Miss Pankhurst and you. When I collect him from his house tomorrow morning he will want confirmation that I delivered both of you safely back to the hotel. I'll be sacked if I can't tell him that. I get paid very well to do as I'm told. There have been two attempts on Sir Norman's life, both from CND activists. I was sent on a long defensive driving course run by the SAS for drivers of high profile UK business leaders, so I'm not totally unprepared.'

Gunn turned to Emma, 'and you?'

'I got the same instructions.'

The meal was every bit as good as Emma had said it would be. Both of them chose oysters as a starter followed by Dover sole for Emma and langoustine for Gunn. She chose crème brulée for dessert and Gunn settled for cheese and biscuits. A bottle of chilled Chablis with their food and coffee afterwards completed the supper. During the meal, Gunn kept the conversation away from the events of the day and encouraged Emma to talk about her life with Universal Switchgear and why she was still single at the age of 32.

'I'm not at all sure that I want to get married,' she confided in Gunn. 'I've had one or two relationships—I believe that's what they're called—but certainly nothing that I wanted to make permanent.' The waiter returned with the bill which Emma took. 'I have my orders from the boss, John. Like Gary, I'll be sacked if I don't hand in a receipt for tonight's dinner.' Their waiter had just returned Emma's business credit card and the receipt when there was the sound of raised voices and a furious struggle in the foyer. Seconds later the restaurant was plunged into stygian darkness. The lights came on again to reveal a bloodied Gary by the double glass doors leading from the foyer into the restaurant. Gunn grabbed Emma's hand and led her out to the foyer.

'Sorry boss that was the best I could do . . . .' Gary stammered gasping for breath. 'He's still out there in the grounds of the restaurant . . . .' another pause to catch his breath . . . . 'he had a rifle and was aiming it at you so I switched off all the lights . . . . I think he's knocked out the receptionist.'

'Other than the blood I can see, how badly hurt are you?' Gunn asked.

'No . . . . no . . . . I'm OK, but he's still out there. I did get in one punch on his nose so he may be bleeding as well.'

Gunn removed the Glock 26 from his ankle holster and handed it to Gary. 'Well done Gary. Take this and stay with Emma. There's no safety catch. Just aim and shoot. OK?'

'OK boss.'

Gary took the Glock automatic and Gunn left him with Emma as he went out into the grounds leaving the hiatus in the Happy Sole behind him.

Emma had explained that the restaurant had been a large private house before being converted firstly into a guest house and then a restaurant. It appeared to be surrounded by fairly extensive grounds and Gunn recalled that they had arrived via a fairly long drive after turning off the main road. No car had left the restaurant car park since the gunman's attempt to kill him, so he—and Gary had said it was a 'he'—must still be in the restaurant's grounds and making his way back to the road where, no doubt, he had left a car or motorbike—the latter more likely. These thoughts went through Gunn's mind as he left the gravelled area which surrounded the building and, hugging the deep shadow of the trees and bushes surrounding a lawn, made his way towards the road. He paused to listen. There was still considerable noise of raised voices coming from the direction of the restaurant and then, ruining his attempt to listen, came the siren and lights of either an ambulance or police car. He was just about to move when there was the unmistakable sound of a human 'sniff'. Had Gary given the gunman a bloody nose? Gunn wondered, and then it was repeated and it wasn't very far away from where Gunn was concealed by a laurel or rhododendron bush. He removed the Glock 17 from its holster and screwed the silencer into the barrel.

'Let's try the old trick,' Gunn thought to himself as he carefully bent down and ran his left hand over the ground by his feet. Was that a stick lying on the ground or was it still attached to the bush and would it give his position away if he moved it? Very gently he grasped the stick and moved it. It came away in his hand without shaking the bush where he was concealed. He swapped hands taking the gun in his left and then with his right hand threw the stick into the undergrowth on his left, away from where he reckoned the sniffing gunman was concealed. The stick made a very satisfying noise and after a brief pause, a figure appeared out of the bushes on Gunn's right with a rifle held across his midriff ready to fire.

'This one's going to talk,' Gunn said to himself as he took careful aim with the Glock. 'Very embarrassing for BID if it's the local gamekeeper out shooting foxes.' Gunn fired twice; right shoulder and left leg. The rifle fell from the gunman's grasp. Gunn removed the silencer from the Glock and walked over to the man who was lying immobile on the lawn. He picked up the rifle. He had no idea who the man was or if he was a professional hit-man. But whatever the man was, his weapon was certainly one used by a professional—a Steyr-Mannlicher 308 calibre with an image-intensifying sight. He slung the rifle over his shoulder and walked back to the restaurant, leaving the gunman where he had fallen.

'Ah, Mr Gunn, you certainly enjoy keeping us busy. Inspector Ross, Thames Valley Police. That looks like a nasty weapon. Shall we look after it?'

'Thank you Inspector. The gunman is lying on the lawn over there,' and Gunn waved his arm in the direction from which he had just come. He's wounded, but alive.'

'Sergeant Ross, take that rifle and get McBain and Clifford to help you with the gunman.' The inspector then turned to Gunn. 'I think we have the gist of what happened in the restaurant. This man certainly saved your life,' he nodded towards Gary. 'The gunman fired, but was distracted by the lights going out. We've found where the bullet went. It very nearly killed another of the diners here tonight.'

A breathless Sgt Ross returned to the restaurant. 'He's dead sir,' he told the Inspector. 'I think he's taken some sort of suicide pill.'

*

'Inspector Ross and the Thames Valley Police were able to identify the gunman—Rudi Brandt by name—a highly undesirable German criminal. He's wanted in a handful of EU Countries and the USA for armed robbery and murder, and so once again the opportunity to identify who it is who wants to get rid of me has been lost,' Gunn replied in answer to Emma's inquiry. Gunn had been told the identity of the gunman in a conversation with the Inspector before they left the Happy Sole. Gary Prescott, their driver, had claimed that he was perfectly fit to drive and, as directed by Sir Norman, dropped both Gunn and Emma off at the Plaza Hotel.

'As I wasn't allowed to buy you supper can I buy you a nightcap as it's still relatively early,' Gunn offered as the two of them walked into the hotel.

'Yes, love one please; single malt with just a little water. I'll meet you in the bar,' and Emma headed for the toilets in the hotel's lobby.

The bar was full and fairly noisy. The seminar or 'workshop' which was being hosted at the hotel had clearly just finished. Gunn paused before ordering their drinks as he saw Emma enter the bar. She wrinkled her nose at the hubbub of noise as she came over to him.

'Have you ordered, John?'

'After tonight's excitement I didn't think this would appeal.'

'Dead right, let's go and raid the mini bar in your room,' and Emma put her arm through Gunn's and the two of them left the bar and headed for the lift. As the doors closed she turned to him and the two kissed. All too soon the lift stopped and the doors opened. At the door to 215 Gunn checked that the little piece of paper he had left in the hinge side of the door was still there. It was; no unwelcome visitors. He opened the door and the two of them went into the room. The door closed behind them and he put his arms round Emma, cupping her breasts in his hands. She sighed with pleasure, dropped her arms down, pulled up her dress and then took his right hand from her breast and placed it in her groin.

'I took my knickers off in the loo as I was so wet,' she murmured as Gunn's hand gently stroked her warm, wet erect clitoris making her breath come quicker and quicker. 'Oh god that's good! Please undress and fuck me really hard, John.'

And so he did.

*

'How the fuck did your useless kraut gunman manage to screw up such a simple task? No, don't answer that. At least we can be grateful that he took the cyanide pill.'

'It was a choice of that or extradition to the USA where he would have spent the rest of his life in prison. It was the MD's driver who saved Gunn this time. He's at Universal for another two days and then goes to Pakistan. That's something that must be prevented.'

'No use telling me that. If your guys had done their job properly this would never have happened.'

'How's Gunn getting on with the delightful Emma?'

'She's with him in the hotel now.'

'If Gunn can't be prevented from going to Pakistan then you might like to send Emma out there as well . . . .'

'On what pretext?'

'Oh for fuck's sake man, use your imagination . . . . a marketing drive on the sub-continent . . . . a reward for successful marketing . . . . a holiday . . . . use your nous man. That'll distract him and make him more vulnerable.'

'Who'll be controlling Gunn in Pakistan?'

'Stephanie Travis.'

'Any good?'

'Moderate, I'd say . . . . yes very moderate.'
'Is there any mileage . . . .'
'The answer's no . . . . don't even think about it.'
'Make contact same time tomorrow?'
'Yes . . . . and for a change, try to have some good news for me.'
'I'll do that.'

CHAPTER 12

When Gunn awoke the next morning just after seven, the space in the bed beside him was empty, but still warm. Emma had slipped out of the hotel an hour earlier and taken a taxi back to her house in Walton Park on the east side of Milton Keynes. While he was shaving his cellphone rang.

'It's Steph, John; sorry for the early call, but I wanted to catch you before you set off on your visit to Universal Switchgear. Would it be possible to meet up this evening?'

'Yes, of course; why don't you take the train up here, have supper and stay the night. I'll reserve a room for you.'

'No, that's OK; I'm out of the office this afternoon so if it fits with your programme, I'd like to drive up to Milton Keynes, meet with you at six and leave by seven; would that work?'

'Yes that'll be fine. I'll meet you in the hotel lobby at six.'

'See you then, bye,' and Stephanie Travis rang off.

With one side of his face still covered with foam Gunn paused before continuing with his shaving.

'That lady is not only worried, but frightened. What the hell is going on at BID?' he muttered aloud before continuing with his shaving.

*

Promptly at 8.30 Emma arrived at the hotel to escort him on his second day at Universal Switchgear. The first port of call was the MD's office where Gunn met Dr Helen McPhearson, the

Deputy MD. The visit gave Gunn a chance to make a point of commending the performance of Gary Prescott, the MD's driver.

'Thank you Mr Gunn; your praise is much appreciated. I only hope that the rest of your visit to Universal is less fraught with attempts on your life, but I suppose those risks go with the job. I hope you'll join us for an informal light lunch in our restaurant.'

The rest of the morning was spent going from one part of the factory to another learning more and more about the scope of Universal's manufacturing base. Lunch in the executive restaurant was a simple affair and Gunn and Emma continued with the visit to the factory afterwards. Heightened security was discretely apparent, but did not intrude on the visit programme. Gunn told Emma of Stephanie's visit to the hotel at 6pm. Her cellphone rang just as she was dropping Gunn off at the hotel. It was clear to Gunn that the news she was receiving delighted her.

'Good news?' Gunn asked.

'Yes; I'm off to Pakistan on Monday to head up a marketing drive. That was Martin Whistler, our International Sales Director. I'll be able to keep an eye on you!'

'Well done; see you back here for supper at 7.30?'

'Cool . . . . see you,' and the car pulled away from the hotel portico.

*

Gunn had time to go up to his room, have a shower and put on a clean shirt before going down to the hotel lobby to wait for Stephanie. 6 o'clock passed as did 6.15 with no sign of her.

'Rush hour traffic on the MI I expect,' Gunn muttered to himself. He knew that Stephanie lived at Bricket Wood, just south of the M1/M25 interchange and that she drove into London every day on the M1. By half past six Gunn was worried because she was always on time and if she couldn't make the meeting at 6pm she would have phoned him from her Bluetooth cellphone in the car. He walked through into the lounge where the large flat screen TV was tuned to the BBC early evening news. The news presenter was

Kate Silverton who was reporting on an impending strike called by the National Union of Teachers over pay and pensions. She interrupted her report.

'. . . . I have some breaking news for viewers, particularly those of you intending to drive on the northbound carriageway of the M1 . . . .'

This caught Gunn's attention from idly flicking through the pages of the current copy of Private Eye. He looked up at the screen.

'. . . . at junction four on the northbound carriageway where an HGV lorry has crashed with a car. The carriageway has been closed and there is now a queue for four miles tailing back from the accident. Our reporter Miles Cavendish is at the scene, Miles . . . .'

The picture switched to the carnage caused by the lorry as it veered out of control pulverising one car and ripping up over a hundred metres of the central steel barriers.

'. . . . the driver of the car never stood a chance and was pronounced dead at the scene of the accident by the ambulance crew. The driver of the HGV was seen running from the scene of the accident and the police have issued a description . . . . witnesses said he was white, wearing dark clothing with a hood covering most of his face . . . .'

The cameraman then zoomed the picture onto the crushed car. About the only item that was recognisable before it was deliberately blurred by the news editor was the number plate.

'Oh no!' Gunn groaned to himself as he saw the mangled remains of what was once Stephanie's silver VW Golf. Stephanie had never married and he guessed that she was in her early fifties. She had been a good friend of his although they had never worked together as the sub-continent was out of Gunn's area of expertise and language. He had no wish to contact Richard Preston so he phoned David Simpson, the Head of BID's Espionage Department.

'It's John Gunn, sir. Have you seen the evening news?'

'Thank you John, the Ops Centre has just told me. I'll be briefing the boss very shortly, but do you know if she had a family?

'She never spoke of one. I have one more day in Milton Keynes, but I would like to be involved in any funeral arrangements if they take place before I leave.'

'Of course; thanks for the call.'

'Hi John!' he was greeted by a cheerful Emma who then saw the grim look on Gunn's face as he replaced the cellphone in his pocket. 'Bad news?'

'Yes Em, let's go and have drink as I need to talk to someone about this wretched assignment which has just notched up another death to add to the slack handful that have already occurred. Feel up to it?'

'Yes of course, if it helps.'

They went through to the bar where Gunn ordered two gin and tonics which they took to a corner booth.

'So what was the bad news that you've just had?'

'Stephanie Travis, my controller on this assignment, who was both worried and, I think, frightened about something, was killed on the M1 about an hour ago on her way here. Her car was smashed to pulp by an HGV lorry whose driver ran from the scene of the accident.'

'Oh no, how ghastly . . . . her family . . . .'

'No, she has no family, but she was a really good friend and I believe was coming here to warn me about something or someone connected with this mission. It's quite wrong of me to involve you, but it struck me that after two attempts on my life which very nearly involved you and—rather more relevantly—as you are now going to Pakistan . . . .'

'I'm a good listener so shoot,' Emma encouraged. Gunn took a sip of his drink.

'I was given this assignment while still on holiday in Monaco. The brief was to take the place of another BID agent, Nigel Lucas, who had been killed. He was part of the BID and FCO security and escort duty provided by the Government for a politically important shooting party of Diplomats and Prime Ministers prior to the G20 Conference. This shoot was on the Duke of Cranborne's

Granvil Estate . . . . that's on the western edge of the New Forest in Hampshire . . . .'

'Yes, I know of it . . . has a very popular garden centre . . .'

' . . . . that's the one. Lucas was murdered. He was shot in the head with a 9mm automatic and then his own shotgun was used by the murderer to blow his head off. I think this was done to hide the use of an automatic and make the man's death look like a shooting accident. I think he was murdered because he was caught spying on a meeting between the Pakistani High Commissioner and either his daughter or another person or all three. His daughter was one of the three FCO officers acting as escorts for the Diplomats . . . .'

'How did she get in on the escort scene?' Emma asked.

'Sorry, I must give you all the detail,' Gunn chided himself. 'His daughter, Cala Williamson by name, married a Brit' in the High Commission in Islamabad. She divorced him when he returned to this Country, but she now had dual nationality. She had a good degree from Princeton University in New Jersey so she applied for and got a job as a Third Secretary in the Overseas Trade and Investment Department of the FCO.

'Got it, go on John.' Emma had not touched her drink.

'Last Saturday was the proper event with a rehearsal the week before. It was on the rehearsal that Lucas was murdered. I went down the following Thursday and stayed in the local pub with the intention of getting some local gossip, rumours whatever.'

'And did you?'

'Yes I did, and two attempts to kill me. I had purposely revealed that I was a Secret Service agent to see what, if anything or anyone that might flush out. I searched Cala's room while she was having supper in the pub. I found a 9mm automatic so I assumed that it was she who had shot the BID agent, but now I'm not sure about that. On my first night at the pub, one of the beaters on the shoot who had lived with his parents in Pakistan and who spoke Urdu was murdered,'

'Why for god's sake?'

'I believe it was because he'd also overheard a conversation—probably at lunch where all the VIPs mix with the beaters and keepers—between the High Commissioner and his daughter or this mystery third person and wanted to tell me about it.'

'How was he murdered?'

'He was poisoned with a rare tropical toxin peculiar to the blue ringed octopus and Puffer fish—I think its proper name is Fugu—which is a hundred times more toxic than cyanide.'

'Honestly John, if this wasn't for real I would say that this was a plot from an Agatha Christie novel.'

'Just wait, there's more to come. That same night, my shotgun was expertly sabotaged so that it would have blown my head off if I'd fired it. The next attempt was by one of the assistant gamekeepers—who I suspect was the same guy who fixed my gun. He tried to get me with that same toxin, but failed.'

'Where the hell did he get that stuff and what happened to him?'

'At the time, I suspected that the toxin had come from the Cala woman as I had seen him humping her in the back of her car.'

'I don't believe it!'

'I told you there was more to come. He tried to break into my room at the pub and in the struggle he fell down the stairs and the phial of toxin he was carrying in his hand smashed. The toxin is just as effective by contagion as it is if ingested, injected or inhaled.'

'Did the police arrest Cala?'

'They would have done, but she'd checked out of the pub the evening before. They did arrest her the next day after the shoot. She turned up the next day with a character called Ghalib Malouf. He's an Iranian asylum seeker, but he'd been spotted by BID's counter-terrorism guys in the company of three known terrorists. The police and I thought he was going to kill the Pakistani Prime Minister. Cala's father is known to be a Taliban sympathiser whereas the Prime Minister, a man called Wasem Halabi, is definitely anti-Taliban. We were all concentrating on safeguarding the PM whereas it now seems that it could well have been Cala who was in danger—hence the 9mm automatic. She probably brought Ghalib along as protection. I found him hanging from a tree in one of the woods to be driven. From where I was hiding in the wood I could see both of the Pakistanis and Cala so none of them could have strangled Ghalib and hung him from a branch. Cala was arrested, but later released on police bail. No, the real murderer is alive and well and on that Granvil Estate.'

'It all seems ridiculously complicated, but you told me that Pakistan had asked for help from BID. Why for heaven's sake?'

'Two of their thermo-nuclear warheads have gone missing— believed to be in the hands of the Taliban.'

'Oh shit!'

'That sums it up nicely, but there's more if you've got the patience to listen before we go and have some supper.'

'Of course,' and Emma took the first sip of her drink.

'During the shoot I made a point of meeting Wasem Halabi and chatting with him. When I got back to the office on Monday I was summoned by BID's Director. Wasem Halabi was in his office and had asked for me to go to Pakistan to help Pakistan's Inter-Service Intelligence trace the two missing warheads. The request was subsequently refused by the Head of the Indian sub-continent department because I'm not an Urdu speaker. Another BID agent who spoke Urdu was tasked. That agent was found dead, squashed into a sports bag . . . .'

'That was in all the newspapers,' Emma interrupted.

'. . . . and so I was given the assignment with the cover as a consultant for Universal Switchgear and a three day visit to Milton Keynes. That almost brings you up to date. Since my arrival here on Monday there have been three attempts on my life and my controller, who was on her way to warn me of something, has just been killed.'

'And you believe that this affects me and the decision to send me to Pakistan?'

'I'm certain of it Em. I, or we, have been watched ever since I arrived here. I changed my room at this hotel to avoid any bugging, but that didn't stop the first attempt to get rid of me. This is how I see it and then we'll go and have some supper. I would greatly value your opinion.'

'OK John, shoot.'

'There's a connection between the Cranborne Family and Universal Switchgear—Richard Jardine, a.k.a the Marquess of Purbeck, elder son of the Duke—was here yesterday, or to be more accurate, his car was here. Did he drive the car here or did someone else drive it to make it look as though Richard Jardine had visited your Company? Your MD knew nothing of his visit. There's a connection between Universal and the Head of BID's Indian sub-continent department. There is something very dodgy about that department and the Head of it in particular. I think that's what Steph was coming to warn me about. How did that character manage to get a Guardian Shield security uniform? Bet your life it was because the site Head of that security company had been given a hefty bung to keep his mouth shut. You and I have been under observation ever since the start of this visit. As the Head of Marketing, had you heard anything about this new marketing drive in Pakistan before today?'

'We have marketing initiatives in countries all over the World, but no . . . . today was the first I'd heard of it,' Emma admitted.

'Not strike you as odd?'

'Now you mention it . . . . yes.'

'Although I have no doubt that you would have been selected anyway on merit to head up this marketing drive in Pakistan, I think they want you out there in the hope that it might distract me from my task of finding the missing warheads. That's put bluntly and I . . . .'

'No offence taken, John; I should have been more savvy about the offer. Let's go and eat while I mull over some of that,' and the two of them went through to the hotel dining room.

*

'What's the name of the man in charge of the BID department which has responsibility for the Indian sub-continent?' Emma asked when they had given their orders to the waiter.

'Preston, Richard Preston,' Gunn answered breaking off a corner of the bread roll on his side plate.

'Do you know why Universal Switchgear was selected as your cover for the assignment in Pakistan? I mean there must be many other companies that could have been selected.'

'I understand it was the recommendation of the British High Commission in Islamabad. Why?' They had to pause as their starter arrived—French onion soup for Gunn and Gazpacho soup for Emma.

'I thought it might have been. I was in Islamabad about eighteen months ago—not long after the death of Osama bin Laden. Security was very tight because of the expected Taliban retaliation so we spent quite a bit of time in the secure compound with the High Commission personnel.'

'You say 'we' Em; who was with you?'

'Martin Whistler and a couple of other guys—one from sales and another from my marketing team.'

'OK, go on.' Gunn had finished his soup.

'We were being hosted by a senior member of the High Commission . . . .'

'Can you remember his name?'

'Wait . . . .' Emma removed her iphone from her handbag, called up her contacts and then ' . . . . yes, it was a David Crawford-Slade. I think he was the Counsellor in charge of the Commercial Section of the High Commission.'

'Will he still be there?'

'I should think so. He'd only been there less than a year.'

'That name's familiar. I've read something or seen something on the TV news.'

'Oh, that'll be the drug scandal that shook the High Commission just before our visit. We had a feeling that it had all been swept under the carpet, but your man Crawford-Slade was heavily implicated by rumour and gossip, but nothing proved. He and our man Whistler seemed to be great buddies and that may well explain the selection of Universal as your cover for helping the Pakistan Government.'

Their main course arrived; steak for Gunn and Sea Bass for Emma.

'What does that man Preston look like,' Emma asked when the waiter had gone.

'Why do you ask?'

'There was a third man with Whistler and Crawford-Slade who was never introduced.'

'Late forties, slightly overweight, thinning brownish hair with a very untidy comb-over which . . . .'

' . . . . hangs down on one side,' Emma completed. 'That's him. Preston was the third man of that trio.' At the time of the successful US Seal raid on Osama bin Laden's house, Universal was completing an IT contract at the Pakistan Military Academy in Abbottabad.'

'BID had about four or five agents in that area at the time,' Gunn continued, 'all of which were controlled by Stephanie Travis who speaks . . . . spoke fluent Urdu and Pashtu.'

'Was she in Pakistan at that time?' Emma asked.

'Oh yes . . . she was there for about four months, but would have stayed clear of the High Commission in Islamabad.'

'Why was that?'

'High Commissions and Embassies don't have the best reputation for keeping secrets secret.'

'And what did she look like?'

'Very well preserved fortyish, blonde hair, good figure and if you think you might have seen her as well, she would have been wearing a hijab.'

'I saw a person matching that description on one occasion. She was with Preston very briefly before leaving the BHC compound.'

'I'm more convinced than ever now you've told me this that there is some sort of conspiracy connected to Preston, Whistler and that character in the High Commission, Crawford-Slade. Steph knew, or thought she knew what it was so she was silenced. Whatever it is I don't believe it is connected to the disappearance of two nuclear warheads. I just can't see these three with that sort of radical motive . . . . unless there was a huge financial kickback for them. No, these guys are are in it for the cash . . . . lots of it, so it has to be drugs. What's your take on it Em?'

'It fits. I've only been invited to Whistler's house once. That was before he made a pass at me which I ignored. He's either got loads of private money or he's on the take. His salary wouldn't support the mansion and style of life in which he and his family live. What about Preston?'

'That I don't know . . . . damn, damn, damn,' Gunn swore quietly, 'that would all have been revealed by Steph. No wonder she was removed. Right, so what we've got is three, no four people, I'm including Richard Jardine, who are all connected in some deal. This means, Em, that you are in real danger out there in Pakistan. These four men are afraid that I will find out what they are up to while I help the ISI trace the two warheads.'

'Don't suggest that I pass on the marketing drive as that will make them even more suspicious.'

'You're right. Come on, time for bed. Will you stay tonight?'

'You try and stop me!'

CHAPTER 13

The next morning before breakfast, Gunn put a call through to Samantha Fox in BID's Research Centre on the 14th floor of Kingsroad House. She answered immediately in spite of the early hour.

'Yes John, good morning and how quickly do you need your information?' Samantha joked guessing that it would be a rush job.

'Ten minutes ago would do nicely, no, seriously before midday would be great and whatever you discover please send to me only, no copies to the sub-continent section.'

'OK, what is it then?'

'The Duke of Cranborne and the Granvil Estate; what's the financial situation with inheritance tax. They have the shoot, farm and garden centre, but is the income from those keeping pace with the interest on the outstanding amount of death duties owed to HMRC?'

'Got it, I'll text you; dreadful news about Stephanie. She was a great chum of mine.'

'And me; possibly see you at her funeral.'

Gunn replaced the cellphone in his pocket and went down to breakfast. Emma was waiting in the hotel lobby promptly at 8.30.

The programme for that last day finished at 11, so Emma suggested that they go to her office and discuss any particular aspects which Gunn wished to raise. As they were driving in the buggy back to the main building Gunn asked for a change of plan.

'Do you ever have your office swept to check on any bugging devices?' Gunn asked as they approached the main building.

'Not as far as I'm aware, why?'

'Instead of having coffee in your office, could we go to the nearest place that serves decent coffee.'

'Sure . . . . 'but Emma said no more as she saw that Gunn had his finger in front of his lips. They stopped beside Emma's Audi TT and changed vehicles. Before they got into her car Gunn cautioned her.

'This is a company, Em, which deals in every type of electrical device. I believe that we have been watched and bugged ever since I arrived here so I want to go to a place where there aren't any bugs. Keep the conversation in your car to any mundane topic you can think of.'

'OK John,' and she did just that, chatting about the visit until she stopped by a Prêt à Manger. Coffee was ordered and once that had been collected they sat down in an empty booth. 'Right, what is it you want to say,' Emma asked.

'Next week you and your team go to Pakistan for this marketing drive. I am convinced that you are seen as a threat by this conspiracy and those involved will see your visit to Pakistan as an ideal opportunity to eliminate that threat . . . .'

'. . . . now you're frightening me . . . .'

'. . . . please be frightened because that will sharpen your awareness of what's going on around you. Assume that every place you once thought was private . . . . that includes your house, your office and your car . . . . is bugged. Don't allow yourself to be drawn into any discussion about what has happened this week. Here is my cellphone number,' and Gunn handed Emma a scrap of paper with the number and how to dial it. 'You've seen how indiscriminately people have been murdered who were perceived as a threat, so never assume that wherever you are or what you are doing is safe; check, check and check again. Sorry to sound like a lecturer, but that is how guys in my line of work try to survive. Lecture over, so let's go back to Universal and I'll say my farewells to your boss.'

Emma was quiet on the drive back to Universal, but made a point of keeping all conversation specific to her remit to prepare Gunn for his assignment in Pakistan. After a light lunch in the boardroom where Gunn said his farewells to Sir Norman Stonehouse and Martin Whistler, Emma drove him to the station. Her farewell kiss was full of emotion and a small tear which she brushed away.

'You make sure John Gunn that you return from this assignment,' and she turned and walked to her car without looking back.

*

During the train journey to London, Gunn received the text from Samantha.

> *"I spoke with all my financial contacts in the city, some of whom have taken longer than I had hoped to reply, otherwise I would have met your midday deadline. The Cranborne family lost the majority of its huge fortune during the lives of the 13th and 14th Dukes because of their profligate lifestyle of gambling and suicidal financial ventures coupled with moronic financial planning to cope with inheritance tax. The 15th Duke was in his seventies before he inherited and made little or no effort to reduce the debt. At that stage it came very close to the State taking over Granvil Hall and its estate, but the young 16th Duke, William Jardine successfully pleaded for more time. The outstanding amount owed to HMRC is assessed by my advisers as just short of £1 billion. In order to keep pace with the interest on this debt, the current Duke has been forced to sell off properties in Tuscany, Provence, Antigua and Corfu and to involve his family in farming, the garden centre and shooting. Until a couple of years ago they were just managing to cope with the interest owed to HMRC, but my contacts have told me that within the last year some fairly large payments have been made—amount unknown—to reduce the capital debt and the interest. The Cranborne's don't have any assets other than the Granvil Estate so it seems that the estate income must be doing better than expected. That's it, hope this helps."*

'It does indeed,' Gunn muttered to himself as the train pulled in to Euston Station.

He called in at Kingsroad House, mainly to find out what arrangements had been made for Stephanie's funeral. He learned from Preston's PA, Davina that no replacement for Stephanie had been appointed and that Richard Preston had been out for most of the day. He had left no messages for Gunn. Irritated by the apparent lack of interest in what had to rate as an important assignment assisting a foreign government organisation, Gunn left the PA's office and went up to the 14th floor where he bumped into David Simpson.

'Hello John, you've just saved me coming down to see you. Come into the office,' David continued speaking over his shoulder as they headed for his office. 'You will be as sad as the rest of us about Stephanie's death.'

'I was hoping to find some details about the funeral but apart from Richard's PA the section appears to be deserted. I also wondered who my controller might be.' By now they were in the Head of Espionage's office.

'Take a seat, John. It's like the old adage of the busses—none, followed by three all at once. Apart from the attempts on your life in Milton Keynes, Stephanie's death yesterday on the motorway and no controller available to help you in Pakistan, I've now just learned that Richard Preston has taken time off saying that he's suffering from the symptoms of extreme stress. Have all the arrangements been made for your move to Pakistan?'

'Yes, all done. Stephanie did all that before I went to Universal Switchgear.'

'OK, earlier today I contacted Javed in Islamabad. He will be your controller for this assignment. From now on with this mission you deal directly with me; make sense?'

'Got that; Steph's funeral?'

'On Sunday, 11o'clock, Mortlake Crematorium.

'Any eulogy, flowers and so on?'

'Yes, Sam Fox has sorted all that.'

'Thank you sir,' and Gunn got up and left the office.

*

The phone had been ringing incessantly in 26, Normanton Road, Claygate—a popular residential town for commuters to the south-west of London. Eventually the neighbour in 24, a Mr Samuels, walked round next door and rang the bell. He had met Mr and Mrs Preston on a number of occasions, but any attempt to further a reasonable neighbourly friendship had been politely, but firmly resisted. No one came to the door. Samuels had turned to leave when he thought he would have one last go. He lifted the letter flap in the front door and bent down to shout, but recoiled at the strong gas fumes which assailed his nostrils. Now really concerned, he hurried back to his house where he had left his cellphone and dialled 999.

The police arrived at the same time as the gas engineers. They found Mrs Preston in the bedroom, the back of her head smashed to a pulp by a hammer which was lying on the bed beside her covered in Preston's finger prints. Mr Preston was in the kitchen with his head in the oven and the gas turned on full. Both were dead. Initially it seemed an open and shut case of suicide by the husband after murdering his wife, but a thorough police pathologist discovered no trace of gas in the man's lungs which gave a clear indication that Mr Preston was dead before he was shoved into the oven to make it look like a suicide. It took the pathologist some time to identify what it was that had killed Preston, but with the help of a colleague from London's Hospital for Tropical Diseases they eventually succeeded in isolating what had killed him. A rare toxin from the Blue Ringed Octopus was the culprit.

*

'Gunn.'
'John, its David Simpson. When are you leaving?'
'Monday.'
'Are you going to Steph's funeral.'

'Yes sir, what's this all about?'

'Richard Preston and his wife have been murdered. The murderer used the same poison that you encountered in Lower Shalford.'

'Tetrodotoxin.'

'That's the one. Apart from letting you know of Preston's death I wanted to warn you to be extra vigilant as the death toll with this assignment is reaching pandemic level. One of Michael Carrington's Counter Espionage teams will be doing a thorough sweep of the area surrounding the cemetery and chapel.'

'Thanks for the warning sir.' Once the Head of Espionage had rung off, Gunn made a number of calls and then dug out his backpack and sorted out what he would take with him to Pakistan.

*

'Did Preston have to be killed.'

'Yes, he'd lost his nerve and wanted 'out' from 'Breakback'. There wasn't an option in this case, it was either that or we would all be spending the rest of our lives in a maximum security prison. I hardly think that your Vanessa would enjoy a prolonged stay in Holloway for her part in the scheme of things.'

'Richard was fine until a week or so ago. What suddenly made him lose his nerve?'

'I believe that it was a combination of circumstances. His failure to prevent BID's involvement in the Granvil Estate shooting party, the failure to get rid of Gunn, the death of Travis and the final straw was the tip-off from a colleague of his in the City who warned him that enquiries were being made about the financial state of the Cranborne family, vis à vis death duties.'

'Not good news.'

'Indeed; let's make sure that Gunn never gets to Pakistan. I'm using the same asset who disposed of Lamb so successfully.'

'Who's that?'

'He doesn't have a name. He's known as the 'Contractor'.

'Why wasn't he used up in Milton Keynes?'

'Because he was away in Paris on contract to the Albanian Mafia removing a witness who was due to give evidence in the trial of Kushtrim Kaja, a Mafia Don.'

'So we have him for this job and everything's fixed for Sunday.'

'Everything.'

*

Barely 200 yards from the concrete enclosure of the Council waste and recycling tip on the west bank of the Thames are the landscaped gardens of Hammersmith Cemetery and the Mortlake Crematorium.

'A cynic might comment that both provide a very similar service,' were David Simpson's thoughts as he scanned the email brief and diagram circulated by Samantha Fox to all Heads of departments in BID. The Director of BID and his two deputies, who headed up the Espionage and Counter Espionage Departments, had all signified their intention to attend the funeral.

The grounds of the cemetery bordered the River directly opposite the boathouses on the other side where the Boat Race VIII removes the sweep shell from the water after the gruelling annual battle between Oxford and Cambridge. All of this background information was included in Samantha's brief which BID's Director was reading in the back seat of the black Range Rover in which he was being driven to the funeral. In the front passenger seat was a bodyguard from CE2, BID's counter-terrorist command. The Director's cellphone rang.

'Yes.'

'Please go secure.' The Director recognised the voice of Michael Carrington, his Deputy Director of Counter Espionage.

'Yes, now secure.'

'All preparations to secure the cemetery and the area around it are now complete. The Met has been very helpful and our operatives have been reinforced by the SO15 police from the Met's Counter-Terrorist Command.'

'Thank you for that. Is Gunn taking any special precautions as he is clearly the target?'

'Yes, I'll brief you when we meet at the chapel.'

'Thank you Michael,' and the Director ended the call.

*

The third Sunday in October was dry with a brisk easterly wind breaking up the surface of the Thames into choppy wavelets as it competed against the ebbing tide. By 10am all the BID and Metropolitan Police counter-terrorist personnel were in position, one hour ahead of the time for the funeral service and cremation of Stephanie Travis. Normally, the crematorium planned on taking bookings for cremations every 40 minutes from 10am to 4pm, but at the request of BID there were no other cremations scheduled for that Sunday.

The turning off the South Circular leading to both the Council tip and the crematorium ended in a mini roundabout after 50 yards—right led to the crematorium and left to a residential estate and the tip. The traffic police were allowing cars through the left turn, but only permitting a right turn to those on the official funeral list.

*

Jak Tosca, the self-styled 'Contractor', had been in the grounds of the crematorium since 5.30 am. He had made a thorough reconnaissance of the whole area 48 hours previously. Correctly assuming that the police would close off the normal access to the cemetery from the South Circular, he had climbed over the locked ornamental gates at the access off the A316 and hid in one of the many large trees to avoid the sweep conducted by the security services. He had also rightly assumed that dogs would be used so he laid false trails with a cloth soaked in aniseed and paraffin which he then threw into the river. His escape route would be over the low metal railings which surrounded the crematorium, across the public tow path and lastly a swim across the river. He had checked the tide tables and at midday it would be dead low water Springs with a very easy swim in his wet suit across barely 30 metres of what was left of the river to the boathouse where he had parked his Ducati Monster 796cc sports bike. He had assembled his 5.56 calibre Colt Delta M16A4 sniper rifle with its times 9 magnification armoured telescopic sight and fitted the long 32 round magazine to his 9mm Uzi parabellum 'grease gun'—the former for a long range shot and the latter for a close quarter kill. He studied the photo of John Gunn. His instructions were to watch for a woman wearing a red coat and head scarf and carrying a red umbrella. She would identify the target male for him. The information which he had been given emphasised his height at 6 foot 3 inches. He had selected his fire position to which he would move at 10.30 am. His fee for this kill was £100,000—half in advance which had been paid into his Cayman Island's account and half on successful completion of the contract; the emphasis in the contract had been on 'successful'. Shooting the wrong target wasn't an option. Everything was ready, now it was just a matter of waiting.

*

The chapel had a maximum seating capacity for 80 people. By 10.20 all the pews were full and it was standing room only for those arriving after that time. Sir Miles Thompson, the Director of BID was standing outside the chapel's portico which was where the hearse would bring Stephanie's coffin. He was talking with his two deputies, David Simpson and Michael Carrington, and greeting the many friends and colleagues attending the funeral and cremation. Both Carrington and the Met Chief Superintendant had tried to persuade him, without success, not to position himself in such a vulnerable place. Sir Miles turned to Chief Superintendant Frobisher.

'Any success with the sweep of the grounds Chief Superintendant?' the Director asked.

'Afraid not, sir.'

'It would be a nice feather in your hat if you got this man as Interpol and half-a-dozen European police forces have been trying to arrest him for more than five years.'

'We believe he's been responsible for at least three murders in London during the past year,' Frobisher offered.

'So I understand . . . . good morning Davina,' the Director had interrupted himself, 'that's a colourful outfit. It adds some colour to what is a rather sombre occasion.' There was no response from the PA to the late Richard Preston.

'Will the precautions work?' David Simpson asked.

'I sincerely hope so . . . . ah! here's the hearse.'

The black Jaguar hearse drove round the roundabout in front of the chapel and slowly entered the portico. Behind it another stretched limousine black Jaguar pulled up short of the portico behind the hearse. The rear doors opened and four men, identical in height, clothing, hair colour, facial hair and dark glasses got out and walked forward to the hearse to extract the coffin from the open tailgate.

'Which is Gunn?' Carrington asked.

'Impossible to say,' the Director murmured, 'as the Judas from within BID has also discovered.' He referred to Davina Newton in her bright red coat, headscarf and umbrella, who was standing with some other BID staff outside the portico. She had to watch, impotently, as the four identical men lifted Stephanie's coffin onto their shoulders and carried it into the chapel.

'Phase one successful,' the Director commented. 'Phase two will be much riskier,' as he and his deputies entered the chapel.

CHAPTER 14

When the last of the BID hierarchy had entered the chapel, Chief Superintendant Frobisher turned to the Sergeant in charge of the Dog Support Unit.

'Sergeant Andrews, which dogs did the first sweep of the grounds?'

'German Shepherds—attack dogs, sir.'

'Do you have the EOD-trained dogs with you?'

'Yes sir, they only arrived an hour ago as they were clearing a suspected terrorist flat in Kilburn.'

'Which is your best sniffer dog?'

'A black Labrador called Guinness, sir.'

'I think there's only one area from which a gunman could get a shot at a member of the congregation and that's from that area over there,' and the Chief Superintendant pointed to some thick undergrowth and bushes to his half right. 'Take your Labrador . . . .'

'Guinness sir.'

'Take Guinness over there and let him have a good sniff around. I think I'm right in saying that your sniffer dogs are trained to ignore false lures and scents.'

'That's right sir, we'll get him over there right away,' and Sergeant Andrews hurried over to a police van emblazoned with the logo 'DOG SUPPORT UNIT', opened the back door and released a black Labrador who was sent to scour the area identified by the Chief Superintendant.

*

Jak Tosca had moved to his selected fire position at 10.50. His false scent trail had proved remarkably effective as the dogs had all disappeared off in the direction of the river. He had been told that the target would be one of the pall bearers and the red-coated woman would point to him with her umbrella. He identified the woman and raised the butt of the Colt assault rifle into his shoulder. The four pall bearers got out of the car following the hearse; four identical men to the last detail.

'Shit!' he mouthed, 'and I've been dropped right in it. They've known all along what was planned.'

But by then all four men had gone into the chapel. He knew that the longer he waited the more vulnerable he would become. It should have been two quick head shots and then away on his escape route across the river.

'Looks like my second plan will have to be used.'

Three days previously when he had done his reconnaissance of the crematorium, he had arrived on a scrambler motorbike which he had hidden in the bushes close to his fire position. He had then returned to London by bus and this morning had come on his Ducati which he'd parked at the boathouse.

People started to appear from out of the portico. Once again he raised the butt into his shoulder and looked through the sight. There she was—the woman in red with her umbrella and standing right next to the four pall bearers. Tosca's finger tightened on the trigger.

'WOOOOOF!'

A loud, deep bark right behind Tosca, involuntarily made his finger tighten on the trigger. The rifle fired and the red-coated woman's head disappeared in a spray of blood, bone and brain matter as the soft-nosed 5.56mm bullet disintegrated on impact. Right behind Tosca, and almost sitting on his feet was a large black dog with tail wagging, indicating to his handler that he had done his job.

Tosca leapt to his feet, threw away the rifle and ran to the bike hidden in the bushes. A policeman with the dog handler tried to tackle him, but was brushed aside. The Uzi was still hanging round his neck as he dragged the bike out of the bushes, pulled on the helmet, kicked the starter and roared out of the undergrowth across the roundabout towards the road leading to the South Circular.

*

Gunn had been spattered with the blood, bone and bits of Davina's shattered head seconds before the helmeted gunman hurtled out of the bushes and raced across the roundabout in front of the chapel. He threw off the jacket of the dark suit and the stab vest he had been wearing along with the other three pallbearers and sprinted after the scrambler bike as it disappeared down the road leading to the waste site and the South Circular.

Seventy yards in front of him the gunman tried to turn left at the mini roundabout, but it was blocked by police patrol cars and Armed Response police. The other side of the road was blocked by cars which had exited from the waste site but could go no further because of the police barrier. The entrance to the housing estate was also blocked by police patrol cars so the gunman spun to the right on his bike and roared into the waste site, over the weighbridge, looking for an exit to the river.

There was no exit.

He was surrounded by three huge earth-moving monster machines with large front-acting buckets and blades used to pile up the waste and load it into the 40 ton lorries. Waste site workmen in hard hats and orange jackets were waving and swearing at him. With his left hand he pulled the UZI round and loosed off a spray of bullets in their direction which stopped any further interference from that source.

Once again he spun round and headed back for the exit which was blocked by those cars, now lined up nose to tail, waiting to get out of the site. Pausing only for a split second, the gunman revved the bike and then, like a cross-country scramble, drove the bike up onto the line of cars and used them as a bridge as he bounced from one to another to get out of the site.

*

Gunn reached the mini-roundabout and heard the commotion and shots coming from the direction of the waste site. On his left, the police blocking the exit to the main road were also shouting a warning, only a fraction of a second before Gunn heard the high-revving engine of the bike as it bounced over the cars towards Gunn. And then it screamed into view, taking off over two cars and heading straight for Gunn; its rider holding the throttle on the right handle bar and the Uzi grease gun in his left hand, spraying bullets in the direction of the patrol cars. Gunn dropped to one knee to reduce the size of the target facing the gunman, raised the Glock in both hands and fired a double tap aimed at the helmeted head of the rider. The bike and rider flew over the last car and landed just a few yards in front of Gunn.

'Oh fuck! I've missed the sod!' he swore as he threw himself to one side to avoid the bike roaring headlong towards him. The gunman fell from the bike and the machine skidded on past Gunn on its side with rear wheel still spinning. There was no movement from the gunman. Gunn walked over to the inert rider, his automatic held ready to use if necessary. The Armed Response police emerged from behind the patrol cars. One of them shouted at Gunn to drop his gun. He ignored the man, bent down by the rider and removed the helmet.

There were two bullet holes, right in the middle of the man's forehead.

'That'll do,' Gunn said aloud as he stood up and re-holstered his Glock.

*

By 8.55 all those personnel summoned to the Director's meeting in the BID conference room on the 14th floor were seated. At 9 o'clock Sir Miles Thompson, the Director, entered the conference room. The room was equipped with all the latest gadgets for video, surround sound, map and screen displays and was audio-isolated from the fabric of the building in which it was constructed to prevent any bugging.

The Director sat in the middle of the bowed, long-side of the rectangular table, Angela, his PA opposite him and his two Deputies—Espionage and Counter Espionage—on either side of him. There were ten other people attending the meeting which included the Head of BID's Communication Centre, Commander Stancombe, Head of the Met's Counter Terrorist Command and Assistant Directors from the various Counter-Espionage teams covering terrorism, drugs, immigration, fraud, diplomatic protection and cyber crime—and John Gunn. The Director wasted no time with pleasantries, but got straight down to business.'

'I'll start by thanking Ms Fox for a plan, which some of us thought too risky, which succeeded in removing one of Interpol's most wanted assassins. I must add to that my thanks to Commander Stancombe of the Met's Counter-Terrorist Command for volunteering two of his tallest constables to assist in the guise as pallbearers of Stephanie Travis's coffin. There's only one other person to introduce as the Directorate is now left with no department covering the Indian sub-continent. As a temporary expedient I have asked Sir Thomas Beecham, the recently retired High Commissioner in New Delhi and a previous Deputy Head of Mission at the High Commission in Islamabad to join us. He is fluent in both Hindi and Urdu. Thomas, you are most welcome, but now, business.'

'John Gunn leaves this evening for Islamabad at the request of the President of Pakistan to assist with the investigation into the disappearance of two nuclear warheads—possibly handed over to the Taliban. The reason for the request for a British agent is to have someone on the investigation team of Pakistan's Inter-Service Intelligence, who is not tainted with any connection to the Taliban or any other extreme Islamic group. Gunn will be controlled by our in-country agent.'

'The loss of the nuclear weapons is extremely worrying, both for the NATO forces in Afghanistan and the Israelis who have been warning the UN forum that an event like this was almost inevitable. But running in parallel with the search for the nuclear weapons is another investigation into the death of Richard Preston, BID's Head of the Indian sub-continent department, his wife, his controller, Stephanie Travis and, yesterday, his PA, Ms Newton. These two totally separate investigations are linked by a shooting party on the Duke of Cranborne's Estate where one of our agents was murdered just a fortnight ago. The attempted assassination of another of our agents yesterday is part of the latter investigation and, we believe at this stage, has no connection to the missing nuclear weapons.'

'These two investigations have now prompted questions from the Prime Minister who, understandably, wants to know how many more people will be killed before they are solved. You all have a copy of the report written by John Gunn which covers all the events in which he has been involved. Please make your self familiar with this report so that no time is wasted downstream in this investigation.'

'In spite of the deaths of Mr and Mrs Preston, Stephanie Travis and Davina Newton, Preston's PA, there is still a mole within this building and information is being leaked. That leak must be stopped!'

This statement by the Director focused everyone's attention and a dropped pin could have been heard.

'Thank you everyone.'

*

'I thought you said that this Tosca character was guaranteed to finish the job. That bloody shambolic performance at the Mortlake Cemetery has set us back £50,000 and we're no further forward in safeguarding Operation Breakback.'

'At least he wasn't arrested and questioned. I suppose we can thank Gunn's marksmanship for that small plus in what I agree was a big fat minus. Gunn will be off to Pakistan tonight. Do we know his flight details?'

'Don't even think about wiping out a jumbo load of passengers just to remove him. We have his flight details which Stephanie Travis arranged. Davina passed those to us.'

'Any plans to remove him before he gets on the flight?'

'Yes, that's sorted. I'm going to do it myself this time and it won't cost us a penny. He's on the BA flight to Islamabad departing at 2140 tonight.'

'What'll you use?'

'Ricin . . . . it'll take effect after the flight's taken off.'

'Right, let me know when it's done.'

'Roger to that.'

*

When the meeting finished, Gunn went back to his temporary office in the sub-continent department and picked up his backpack. The new Assistant Director, Sir Thomas Beecham poked his head round the door.

'Anything I can do before you go, John?'

'Thanks sir, but Stephanie was highly efficient in sorting out the admin details so it's just up to me to follow instructions.'

'I don't know if I'm allowed to wish you 'good luck'. In the theatre it's always 'break a leg', oh yes and please drop the 'sir'. Awful waste of time really; I'd be very happy with Tom.'

'Thanks s . . . . Tom. I'm sure that Javed will keep you informed of events in Pakistan,' and Gunn shook hands with the Ex-High Commissioner and left the office. He walked along the corridor to the lifts where he saw several people he knew and exchanged pleasantries. Somewhere in the building there was a mole passing on information about him. Davina was now dead, but the leak had not stopped. He wanted his fellow BID employees to see him leave the building. By the time the lift had reached the ground floor it was empty except for him. There was no one waiting for the lift so Gunn pressed the 15 button. On the 15th floor Gunn pressed the G button and nipped out of the lift as its doors were closing. He walked into the deserted BID heliport where the senior pilot, Malcolm Springfield was waiting for him.

'Got everything?' Malcolm asked as the two walked out to the Lynx helicopter.

'Reckon so . . . . pre-flight checks?'

'Done . . . . so start up as soon as you're ready.'

The Lynx took off from its heliport on the roof of Kingsroad House and headed north—to Birmingham Airport and the 18.30 PIA Flight to Benazir Bhutto International Airport at Chaklala, 18kms from the Capital of Islamabad.

*

At 19.30 that same evening, the BA receptionist at the Information desk at Heathrow Terminal 5 was approached by a man who wanted to know if a colleague who was travelling on the 21.40 flight to Islamabad had already checked in. The man said he had a letter which he wanted his colleague to take to Pakistan. The receptionist checked her VDU.

'No sir. There's no one with that name on the British Airways 21.40 flight.'

The man walked away and swore loudly. Had he not walked away without looking back he might have seen the receptionist pick up the phone.

'Oh hi Frances, I've just had that inquiry you mentioned,' and then a pause as she listened. 'Yes, he wanted to know if a Mr J Gunn had already checked in for the BA 21.40 Flight to Islamabad; 'another pause and then, 'yes I operated the desk-cam and I'll email the photo over to you, bye.'

*

At about the same time as the inquiry at the information desk in Terminal 5, Pakistan Airways Flight PK 6540 flew over the small town of Babol on the southern shore of the Caspian Sea at 33,000 feet. John Gunn was fast asleep in his business class seat.

CHAPTER 15

The interior of the impressive circular, domed Jinnah Convention Centre had been stripped of all its seating to make room for the myriad of stands representing worldwide international engineering companies. Of these by far the majority were those companies from China and South Korea. Universal Switchgear had been allocated a prominent position, probably, Emma reckoned, because of the company's reputation with high quality submarine fibre-optic communication cables.

Emma had been in Islamabad since the weekend and after a hectic 48 hours of getting all the equipment onto the stand—some of which had arrived late with American Airlines Cargo Carriers because of an engine refit at Heathrow—she and her marketing team now had a full programme of interviews with prospective customers. The only time that she had seen Martin Whistler, her boss, was when the British High Commissioner, Sir Alan Thomas had visited the exhibition after the opening ceremony by Pakistan's President, Azil Zadari. He had been accompanied by the Commercial Counsellor, David Crawford-Slade and the Defence Attaché, Brigadier Hamish McCulloch. Emma had been signally unimpressed by the oily and condescending manner of the Counsellor and the obese and whisky-smelling Defence Attaché who she thought looked utterly ridiculous in his kilt. In contrast, she was looking particularly attractive in a smart business outfit which included a scarf to cover her head in deference to Moslem custom.

Emma checked her watch; very shortly she would be able to hand over to her very efficient deputy, Louise Milburn, and then she could take a break and a coffee 'to die for' in the staff restroom well away from the exhibition concourse. She had politely declined a whisky-laden breath from McCulloch inviting her to dinner before giving the Counsellor a concise and brief summary of what Universal expected to achieve by the end of the industrial expo. His only response was a feeble pat on the shoulder as though she was a five-year-old child.

She made her way through the throng of visitors to the expo to the small restrooms at the far side of the circular concourse. Each major exhibitor had a room with its own toilet and wherewithal to cook a snack in a microwave or brew up tea and coffee. She punched out the code on the lock and pushed the door open. She was grabbed roughly from behind, her headscarf was pulled over her face while her arms were pinned behind her and a chloroform pad was held across her mouth and nose. Her last thoughts as she started to lose consciousness where John's advice to her . . . . 'suspect everyone, don't assume that any place is safe. Check, check and check again' . . . . and then a roaring vortex and darkness.

*

Flight PK6540 landed at Islamabad International Airport at 06.30 hrs local time. It was only just over a year since Osama bin Laden had been killed by the US SEAL raid on his compound in Abbottobad and visitors from the USA and Europe, in particular, were warned by their respective foreign affairs offices to avoid Pakistan unless really necessary. Gunn was deeply tanned from his holiday in Monaco and made a point of speaking in Arabic to match his alias of Jaafor Ghasaan as he went through Passport Control. The Captain of his PIA flight from Birmingham had proudly told the passengers that in a very short time all flights would land at the brand new airport which was being built at Fateh Jang as the current airport could no longer cope with the quantity of passengers it was currently experiencing. Gunn had nothing to pick up from the carousel at baggage claim so was one of the first passengers to exit to the arrival area.

He slung the backpack over one shoulder and walked out of the arrival concourse to the taxi ranks. He greeted the taxi driver in Arabic and requested the Marriot Hotel in Aga Khan Road—a hotel in the Shalimar District of the City used by the majority of businessmen and diplomats visiting the Capital of Pakistan. In 2008 it had been the target of a lorry bomb which exploded in front of the building leaving a twenty foot deep crater, 54 people dead and 260 injured—most of whom were Pakistanis. His taxi driver answered his request in a mixture of Urdu, Arabic and Pashtu which Gunn found fairly easy to understand.

Gunn paid off the driver in US dollars which was still the most acceptable form of currency whether you were a Jihadist, Imam or hotel bell-boy. The reception counter ran the full length of the left side of the lobby and all the receptionists were busy either checking in or checking out the clientele. The arrangement he had fixed with Javed Iqbal before he left London was for him to wait in the lobby of the Marriot Hotel until contacted by a bell-boy.

'Ghasaan sahib?' was asked in perfect English

Gunn turned in the direction of the inquiry which had come from a bell-boy who could not have been older than 15.

'Yes, who wants to know?'

'A message from Iqbal sahib,' and a folded piece of paper was handed to Gunn who exchanged it for a dollar note. He unfolded the note.

> *"Go out to the parking area in front of the hotel. Find the black Jeep SUV with the number plate KN 355. Get in. I will be waiting for you. Javed"*

Gunn crumpled the note and put it in his anorak pocket. The marketing team from Universal Switchgear was in the Pearl Continental Hotel and would spend most of the day at the Jinnah Convention Centre where there was an international industrial exhibition. He would have to make contact with the team and its leader, Emma, to authenticate his role as a consultant to the company. He had been cautioned about the risk of staying in a high profile hotel so Javed had made arrangements for Gunn to stay at his house ten miles away in Rawalpindi. Having paused for a few moments while he watched the comings and goings of the hotel guests in the lobby, Gunn walked out of the front entrance, past the covered portico where more guests were arriving in taxis and across to the parking area.

Gunn identified the Jeep, but could see nothing of the interior through the blacked-out windows. He tried the front passenger's door, but it was locked. He sensed, rather than saw the doors open in the car parked beside the Jeep. Turning and ducking low at the same time he avoided a blow from a brutal looking club wielded by one of the two dhoti-clad men who had appeared from the Mitsubishi SUV. Both men wore black face masks. Gunn swung his backpack with all his force behind it, knocking the club from the man's hand and following it with a scything kick to the man's ankles which knocked him to the ground. The man's accomplice had been unable to assist because of the narrow space between the parked cars, but now he rushed forward over the body of his accomplice and straight into a crushing blow from Gunn's newly acquired club. He dropped like a stone giving Gunn time to use the club again on his first assailant to ensure he took no further part in the struggle. The front passenger door opened and the only thing that saved Javed Iqbal from being brained with the club was his shout to warn Gunn. While Gunn had engaged with the two assailants from the Mitsubishi, Javed had taken the opportunity of this distraction to tackle the third assailant in the driver's seat of the Jeep who had been keeping Javed covered with an automatic.

Gunn had been told that there were always police hanging around outside the Marriott because of the number of wealthy and important guests which it attracted. Those police now decided to take an interest in the disturbance that had taken place in the area between the two cars. Fortunately Javed was able to explain that he and Gunn were the target of an attempted mugging, otherwise both of them would have joined the three assailants in the cells at the police headquarters at Shahrah-e-Jamhuriat. The police were only convinced when Javed explained that Gunn was a guest of Major General Rashid Kumari of the ISI and the Country's President. It helped too when he handed over the 9mm automatic with which he had been threatened while the two muggers attacked Gunn.

'Not a very pleasant welcome on your first visit to Pakistan,' Javed commented as he turned onto the road to Rawalpindi.

'I've had worse and you come to expect it in our line of work. We've got leaks at Kingsroad House and it seems you also suffer from that problem after today's episode.'

'There are only three people in the High Commission who are aware of my existence; the Head of Mission, his deputy and the Defence Attaché. One of them is responsible for leaking the details of your arrival and the fact that I was meeting you.'

'Which one, Javed? . . . . you must have your suspicions.'

'I'm almost certain it's the DA . . . . Brigadier McCulloch; an unsavoury character who is a very poor advertisement for the British Army. His wife went back to Scotland after only three months out here and it would seem that he has been swilling whisky morning, noon and night ever since. I'm surprised the High Commissioner puts up with it. That and his grotesque attempts to have affairs with the wives of other officers in the Attaché Corps He's bosom pals with another unsavoury character in the High Commission; Crawford-Slade. He's the Commercial Counsellor and only just escaped being indicted in a drug scandal that came very close to the High Commission. As is usual in these cases, three or four junior personnel in the High Commission were sent back to the UK, but he remained. Ah! Here we are John,' and the Jeep turned into a driveway in front of a bungalow almost swamped in the vivid colours of bougainvillea.

They were met by on the bungalow's veranda by Ayesha, Javed's wife. She was dressed in traditional style in a shalwar kameez while, in contrast, Javed was in western style dress wearing slacks and an open-necked shirt.

'Welcome to Pakistan, Mr Gunn—I think your name is most suitable for your profession. Come in and have some breakfast,' and Ayesha led the way into the bungalow.

*

Gunn had a shower and then joined Javed and Ayesha in the kitchen where the aroma of ground coffee and toast whetted his jaded post-flight appetite. Javed had changed into traditional clothing. They were seated at the breakfast bar and Gunn had just had his first sip of coffee when his cellphone rang.

'May I take the call here in the kitchen, Javed?' Gunn asked. 'It'll save time if you can hear it.'

'Of course, go ahead.'

'Gunn.'

'Is that John Gunn?'

'Speaking.'

'John, it's Louise, Louise Milburn, Emma's deputy on the Marketing Team.'

'Yes Louise, what is it?'

'It's Emma . . . . she's vanished. She went to the rest room to take a break after the opening ceremony and that's the last I saw of her. I told Martin . . . . that's Martin Whistler our boss, but he hasn't done anything to find her. After all the trouble we had back in England before we came here, I'm sure that something's happened to her.'

'You're in the Jinnah Centre?'

'Yes . . . . yes, I'm on the stand. I couldn't phone sooner because Martin was watching me.'

'Got all that Louise, I'll be with you in . . . .' and Gunn glanced at Javed who had heard the contents of the phone call and mouthed 'twenty minutes' . . . . twenty minutes.'

'Oh thanks John,' and she ended the call.

'Right, let's go John. We'll grab your Glocks on the way out. Bye love,' Javed waved to Aeysha as the two men went back out to the Jeep having picked up Gunn's automatics which he put in his backpack.

Lack of traffic and Javed's intimate knowledge of the route got them to the convention centre in just over 15 minutes. Javed had passes for both of them for the whole period of the industrial expo. They made their way through to the central area of the expo, hindered by the throng of people wandering around aimlessly, where they identified the Universal Switchgear stand and a very anxious Louise.

'Thanks so much for coming. I don't know where Martin is . . . . he seems to have vanished as well,' Louise blurted as soon as she saw them. Gunn quickly introduced Javed.

'How long ago did Emma leave the stand?' Javed asked as he took his cellphone out of his pocket.

'About forty minutes ago.'

Javed called up a number on his phone. 'Rashid, it's Javed. I'm at the Universal stand,' . . . . a pause and then, 'fine, we'll wait here for you,' and he ended the call. 'That's General Rashid Kumari who's the head of Inter-Services Intelligence. We had expected something like this which is why he's here. He tried to cancel, or at least postpone this expo as it gives terrorists the ideal opportunity to take Western hostages. It's only a year since the US SEAL raid which killed Osama bin Laden in Abbottobad, which is only some 70 miles north of here. There is considerable resentment that the raid was done without any cooperation or knowledge of this Country's Government or Armed Forces.'

Even as Javed finished explaining who Rashid was, the man himself appeared with two armed soldiers. The General was almost as tall as Gunn, jet black hair and moustache and dressed in the black uniform of the Inter-Service Intelligence. Javed did the introductions.

'Do you have any idea where your Sales Director is Miss Milburn?' the General asked.

'No . . . . no sir . . . . he just . . . .'

But even as Louise answered the General's question, Martin Whistler appeared, took one look at the group talking to Louise, turned and ran, forcing his way through the crowded concourse. The General blew his whistle and his two escort soldiers headed off after Whistler.

'It seems that your Sales Director has some questions to answer. He won't get far I can assure you. All the doors will have been closed—that was the purpose of the whistle,' the General explained to Louise.

No sooner said than done; the General was called on his radio and told Javed, Gunn and Louise that Whistler had been detained and was being taken to the ISI Headquarters in Islamabad.

'Come gentlemen, let us go and find out what Mr Whistler has to say,' and the General led the way through the visitors to the expo. The crowd parted and gave them a clear passage such was the reputation of the ISI.

*

Emma slowly regained consciousness wondering if she had dreamt the nightmare of being hooded, tied and bundled into the back of a car. As she came to her senses it was no nightmare. Her hands and feet were no longer tied and she was lying on a single bed in a sparsely furnished room. She sat up and then immediately wished that she had remained lying down. The floor of the room was concrete and the window had very solid looking vertical bars on the outside of the glass. She rose unsteadily to her feet and explored her surroundings. There were two doors, one was solid wood and locked the other was a composite door and to her amazement led to a bathroom and toilet. There was another window—also barred. She had been desperate to have a pee since she recovered consciousness, so now made use of the lavatory, and again to her surprise the flush worked with vigorous efficiency.

Feeling better by the minute, she removed her business suit jacket and went back into the bedroom and over to the window. The view took her breath away. Whatever building she was in, it was situated high up among what appeared to be the crenellated battlements of some castle which had been built on the rocky high ground overlooking the confluence of two large rivers; one was sapphire blue in colour and the other a muddy brown. In the distance she could just see the early snow on the foothills of the

Hindu Kush mountain range. Pressing her head against the bars and looking to her left, Emma could see that the conjoined rivers flowed through a deep gorge spanned by two modern-looking bridges. She glanced at her watch—another surprise as it was still on her wrist. It was now 1.30. The time reminded her that she had gone to the rest room at the expo to get something to eat. Now she was ravenous as she had not eaten since supper the night before at the Pearl Continental Hotel.

'Hello! Anybody there?' Emma shouted as loudly as she could. Silence; and then she heard the noise of someone or some bodies moving around on the other side of the solid door. The door was unlocked and the barrel of a Kalashnikov assault rifle preceded a tall man in traditional dhoti. He spoke no English, but gestured that Emma should move back from the door; she complied with the gestures. Once she was on the other side of the room, the first man said something and another man came in with a tray covered by a spotless white napkin. 'This looks hopeful,' Emma thought. The tray was placed on the small table in the centre of the bedroom and then both men backed out of the room, closing and locking the door.

Emma removed the napkin to reveal a very neatly presented plate of meat curry with bowls of rice and chapattis and an assortment of chutneys, sauces and side dishes. There was a plastic jug of lemon barley water and a plastic cup. The fork and spoon were also plastic. She pulled the only chair up to the table and set about the meal with gusto. 'I couldn't give a bugger if the food's doped, I'm bloody starving,' she said aloud to the empty room. When she had sensibly finished every scrap of food on the tray having no idea when she might be fed again, Emma retired to the bed and in an instant was fast asleep.

CHAPTER 16

As they drove in convoy with the ISI vehicles, Gunn imagined that the intelligence headquarters would be some grim building like the Lubyanka in Moscow. He was pleasantly surprised when the convoy turned into what looked more like a museum complex with neatly manicured lawns and flowerbeds. The convoy stopped in front of a modern three storey steel and glass building. Javed and Gunn followed the General to an unostentatious office on the third floor which the General claimed as his workplace.

'I realise how anxious you must be gentlemen,' the General began as coffee appeared miraculously and was laid out on a low table. 'We understand that speed is of the essence in these kidnappings if we are to find Miss Pankhurst . . . . alive that is. Sorry to be so blunt, but you will know from the coverage on Al Jazeera that the Taliban and Al Qaeda enjoy the sensationalism of beheading their hostages. Please help yourself to coffee and I will go and see what my men have learned from Mr Whistler.'

Once the General had left and the two men had taken up his offer of helping themselves to coffee, Javed turned to Gunn.

'Did you suspect this man Whistler?'

'I can't pretend that I took an instant liking to him, but in the short time that I was with Universal I would have to have been a detective of Holmesian skill to have discovered enough evidence to suspect him of being involved in any conspiracy. I still don't see the connection between Universal and the two missing nuclear warheads.'

'You aren't alone in your puzzlement about that connection, but perhaps we may learn something shortly. The ISI has a pretty fierce reputation and I think it would be unwise to delve too deeply into their interrogation methods although I am assured by Rashid that the ISI are like angels compared to some of the methods used by the United States in Camp Delta at Guantanamo.'

'After some of the recent revelations by the World media of the cases of US rendition of their prisoners, that doesn't surprise me. But if you're a relative of a victim of a terrorist outrage like the World Trade Centre or the London bombings it certainly colours your judgement on what is and is not an acceptable form of interrogation. In this case with Emma I can't pretend that I would be too fussed if the ISI was fairly heavy handed in its interrogation of Whistler.'

'That's understandable, but I'm certain that one of the lines of interrogation will be to establish if there is a connection between Whistler and Mohammed Ali Qureshi, the Controller of the nuclear storage facility at Khushab.'

*

'That idiot Martin has been arrested by the ISI.'
'On what grounds?'
'He panicked when he saw the ISI with Gunn and Iqbal at the Universal stand.'
'Who alerted Gunn about Pankhurst?'
'It was her sidekick in Universal. Wait, oh yes, a Louise Milburn.'
'Where are they now?'
'Who?'
'Whistler of course.'
'Being interrogated at the ISI Headquarters.'
'It won't take them long to break him.'
'Agreed, that's why I contacted you.'
'We must move the girl immediately. Does Whistler know what we plan to do with the girl?'

'I doubt it, but I reckon that we must assume the worst.'

'Right, move her now; away from the Dak bungalow at Attock Fort and on to Peshawar to the usual meeting place where you are to hand over the woman to Mubashar Ali Munda who controls the Taliban and Al Qaeda in that part of the Tribal Areas.'

'What does he plan to do with her?'

'You would rather not know my friend, but that is her fault for interfering with our financially rewarding line of business. The delivery of a white woman belonging to one of the largest industrial companies in the UK will be worth a huge ransom fee and at least £10million of heroin for us.'

*

Gunn and Javed had been in General Kumari's office for just over 15 minutes when Gunn's cellphone vibrated with the receipt of a text message. It was from BID's Operations Centre and informed Gunn that GCHQ in Cheltenham had intercepted a telephone call from the UK to Pakistan. Gunn read the text copy of the intercepted call just as General Kumari returned to his office.

'We now have confirmation of Whistler's contacts here in Islamabad,' the General announced.

'And from London I've just heard that Emma Pankhurst is about to be moved from Attock Fort where she has been held in a Dak bungalow to Peshawar. Where is Attock and what is a Dak bungalow?' Gunn asked.

'I'll explain in a minute, John. Rashid, did Whistler reveal his contacts here in Islamabad?' Javed asked.

'He was very keen to cooperate when we explained what the alternative might be. The British Defence Attaché and the Commercial Counsellor in the High Commission, Brigadier McCulloch and Mr Crawford-Slade, but we must lose no time gentlemen if they are moving Miss Pankhurst to Peshawar. I have had confirmation that neither of those two men has been seen in the High Commission today. As long as they are outside the High Commission and its compound we can arrest them, but we will choose that opportunity carefully. Our priority is to rescue Miss Pankhurst. Once she is in the hands of the Taliban and Al Qaeda in the Tribal Areas our chances of finding her are very slim. How long ago, Mr Gunn, was that message intercepted by your GCHQ?'

'Just over twenty minutes,' Gunn replied after checking his watch.

'Right, come with me gentlemen,' and General Kumari led the way from his office. They took the lift to the ground floor and then out of the rear of the ISI building to a helipad where a black-painted Aerospatiale Alouette helicopter was parked with rotors turning. The co-pilot/observer held the door open to allow the General, Javed and Gunn to board the helicopter. Once they were all strapped in, the Alouette lifted off and headed west to Peshawar.

*

Emma was woken by the sound of voices raised in argument on the other side of the door to her bedroom. The door was unlocked and four men armed with assault rifles entered the room. She was bustled out of the room into a hallway and then out of the building onto a paved area where three Toyota SUVs were parked. No attempt had been made to blindfold her. Before she was bundled into the back of the middle SUV, Emma had a chance to see her surroundings. The building in which she had been held captive was a well-maintained bungalow built on what might have been the parade ground of a most impressive fort. She kicked herself mentally for not knowing more about the geography and history of Pakistan as she knew that it was vital for her to remember as much as she could about her surroundings if she was to assist any attempt by herself to escape or others to rescue her.

A driver got into the front of the SUV and an armed guard climbed in beside him. Emma was left on her own in the back. At the last minute just before the convoy of three cars headed for the gates leading out of the fort, two men left the bungalow and climbed into the leading SUV. Emma only caught a glimpse of the men, but was certain that one of them was the corpulent figure of the Defence Attaché whom she had seen that morning at the opening ceremony of the Expo.

The convoy of three cars turned right onto the dual carriageway road outside the fort and then crossed the gorge which Emma had been able to see from the window of her bedroom. On the flight out from London, Emma had studied the paperback guide to Pakistan which she had bought at the airport bookstall, but now she wished that she had studied it in far more detail. What worried her was the fact that she had not been blindfolded nor had her watch been removed. She put this down to a couple of options; they either did this out of the kindness of their hearts or it didn't really matter if she saw where she was going as the intention was to kill her when she had served whatever purpose her kidnapping was meant to achieve. She ruled out option one so option two was the most likely event. The cars were on a major road and were going west—she had worked that out by the position of the sun in relation to the time on her watch. The road was obviously a major highway, so perhaps it was the Grand Trunk Road which she had read about in her 'Lonely Planet' guide. Wracking her memory and trying to picture the maps and pictures in the guide she could remember that the Grand Trunk Road crossed Pakistan's major river—the Indus, which was fed by the melting snow of the Karakoram Mountains on the border with China, hence the colour of its vivid icy blue torrent against the silted brown waters of the Kabul River which flowed across the Tribal Areas from the Khyber Pass. She remembered that there had been a piece in the guide about the confluence of the two rivers and the fort which had been built at that point by Akbar the Great in the Sixteenth Century, but for the life of her she couldn't dredge the name of the fort out of her memory.

If it was the Grand Trunk Road then it was likely they were headed in the direction of Peshawar—the guide had described it as a city steeped in 2,000 years of history and bloodshed. Even the guide hadn't pulled its punches referring to it as 'bandit country' where you could buy anything from the blood-stained uniforms of the defeated Russian soldiers from the nine years of Russo-Afghan conflict to a replica pair of Purdy shotguns, a .5" calibre machine gun or an anti-aircraft missile. Emma was well aware that if Peshawar or further west was the destination then she would be well inside Taliban territory and any rescue would be a forlorn hope. No—she had made up her mind. She would have to do something if she hoped to live longer than the next 48 hours.

*

Once they had both got their earphones on, Gunn turned to Javed. 'What is a Dak bungalow and where is this Attock fort?'

'During the time of the British Raj, John, bungalows were built as staging points for mail delivery and overnight accommodation for the civil servants who administered a particular district. Once communications improved and the bungalows were no longer needed for the mail they became very popular with the British who enjoyed trekking in the more remote areas of the Raj. They still exist to this day and are very popular with the tourists as they are an inexpensive way of touring around our Country. The only disadvantage is that even if a tourist has a confirmed reservation, but the bungalow is needed by a district official, the tourist will be told to leave. The fort at Attock, which we will fly over any minute now, was built by Akbar the Great during the time of the Afghan wars in the sixteenth century. It lies at a strategic point where the Indus River and the Kabul River meet. There it is now if you look to your right.'

'And that dual carriageway crossing the river, is that what my Rough Guide described as the Grand Trunk Road?'

'It is and looking at the amount of traffic on it, I doubt if the kidnappers of Emma will be very far ahead of us.'

Javed's tour guide patter to Gunn on the Alouette's internal net was interrupted by the General who had been tuned to an ISI frequency.

'My ISI agents in Peshawar have confirmed that Mubashar ali Munda is expected to arrive there today and the atmosphere in that city is like a pot that is about to boil over. They tell me that a number of CIA operatives have also been identified so it would seem, gentlemen that there could be serious trouble. Are you both armed?' the General asked to which both Javed and Gunn nodded. 'Good, you might well need to use your weapons.'

*

The traffic was really dense which meant that the drivers of the multi-coloured buses and lorries quickly lost patience with waiting in a queue of vehicles and reverted to their fabled practice of driving on the wrong side of the road, weaving in and out of the on-coming traffic in a suicidal manner and overtaking on blind corners and hill crests. On several occasions Emma was convinced there would be a crash—indeed, she hoped that might be a way of escaping from the SUV provided she could survive a head-on collision with a lorry or bus. She imagined that the passengers on the buses would be terrified by the suicidal risks taken by their drivers, but as her SUV and the buses passed in opposite directions it seemed that the passengers revelled in their driver's maniacal driving and she could even hear their cheers as they urged the driver to take more death-defying risks.

Hardly a word had passed between the driver of her Toyota SUV and the armed guard in the front passenger seat. Emma was still in the same clothes in which she had been abducted from the Expo rest-room, less the headscarf. She glanced again at the guard in the front passenger seat. The heat and the boring traffic queues were taking their toll on his ability to stay alert and Emma had seen his eyes close more than once.

'Think, think Emma,' she silently chided herself as she searched for anything that might be used as a weapon. 'Use your brain girl,' she thought as she patted the pockets of her business suit. The majority of the pockets were useless and only for style and decoration, but the side pocket still had her favourite Parker ball-point pen.

The hand-held radio blurted into life which roused her guard out of his semi-comatose state much to Emma's annoyance. The lead SUV had pulled into a lay-by on a stretch of the trunk road that had an abundance of low scrub and stunted Juniper and Cedar trees. Emma tried to see who, if anyone, got out of the lead SUV, but no one appeared. A message came over the radio. The guard got out of the SUV and opened the near-side rear door. He indicated with his assault rifle that she should get out.

'Was this to be her execution?' was the query which went through Emma's mind as he got out of the Toyota. The third SUV had stopped some thirty yards behind the Toyota and all four men had walked over to the trees at the side of the lay-by and were urinating. Her guard indicated with his rifle that she could relieve herself if she so wished. She shook her head and summoned her total grasp of Urdu with 'Shukriya' to thank him for the offer. One of the men in the third SUV said something which made them all laugh.

'If they think I'm going to squat down over by the trees and pee in front of them all, they're sadly mistaken, however desperate I may be,' she murmured and turned back to the car.

Both her driver and the guard were still enjoying whatever joke had been cracked by the men in the other vehicle, so neither of them noticed as Emma deftly flicked the child lock on the back door from 'lock' to 'unlock' and then got back into the rear seat.

The convoy set off once more. After less than five minutes they passed a large sign showing that the highway was dividing—one road going to Peshawar and the other heading for Mardan and the Malakand Pass leading to the North West Frontier Province. The highway was still choked with traffic which meant that the three vehicles were well and truly separated by the jostling and weaving buses and lorries. Emma grasped the Parker biro and removed it from her pocket. Her guard was almost asleep demonstrating his Nation's male contempt for the opposite sex and the possibility that Emma might possess the ability to escape from him. Emma glanced behind her. There was no sign of the third SUV.

Then the perfect opportunity presented itself. There was the loud crunching noise of a crash behind them and the road was immediately blocked with people shouting and waving their arms.

Leaning forward very slightly, Emma could see that the stock of the guard's AK47 was propped against his shoulder with the muzzle resting on his dhoti-covered legs. She had to assume that the magazines were loaded—two of them were taped together—and that the weapon was cocked. She had no idea if there was a safety catch; she just had to hope that this particular character was not safety conscious.

The gap behind them had now extended to about 50 yards. It was now or never and she would kick herself at some unknown time in the future when they were about to execute her for not grasping this chance, however slim it might seem. With the ballpoint held tightly in her left hand, she back-handed it, point first, into the guard's right eye, at the the same time grabbing the stock of the AK47 and pulling it towards her.

The guard screamed in agony as he covered his face with both hands, blood spurting out between his fingers. The driver turned his head to stare into the barrel of the AK47 a split second before Emma pulled the trigger and shot him in the head. The engine of the SUV stalled and it jolted to a halt. The semi-blinded guard screamed with pain and rage as he grasped the barrel of the AK47. Emma pulled the trigger sending the second bullet through his left eye and blowing half his skull out of the open window.

Emma scrambled out of the stationary Toyota, opened the front passenger door and pulled the guard out onto the road and dumped him in the gutter. As he came clear of the SUV, her handbag fell out onto the road. She picked up the bag and put it back on the front seat. A quick glance behind her confirmed that the chaos of the crash continued. The wide central reservation between the east and west carriageways meant that little interest was taken in the stalled SUV by people in the traffic heading in the opposite direction. Emma hurried round to the driver's door, opened it and pulled the driver out onto the road. With some difficulty, she dragged the driver round to join the guard. She then got back into the driver's seat, quickly checked her bag and was amazed to find her cellphone and its charger still there, together with her purse and wallet. She put the gear lever in neutral, restarted the engine and drove away to catch up the tail end of the queue which they had been following since leaving Attock.

Ahead of her, Emma saw the large sign showing the up-coming split of the Grand Trunk Road—straight on and west to Nowshera, Peshawar, the Khyber Pass and Afghanistan, right turn and north to Mardan, the Malakand Pass, Swat and the North West Frontier Provence.

Emma followed the signs leading off the highway to the left which then went up a ramp onto a bridge over the road she had just left and on to the northern highway where there was considerably less traffic. Somewhere below and behind her were the two dead men and other two SUVs. Beside her on the passenger's seat was the AK47.

CHAPTER 17

'Mahmood, this is Brigadier Sahib. I can't get Shafiq on the radio. Can you see the car with Shafiq and the woman in front of you?'

'No Sahib. There is bad accident in front of us and we cannot pass.'

'Oh shit! That would have to happen,' the Defence Attaché cursed and then addressed the driver of his SUV. 'Pull over to the side of the road, Farooq . . . . no! You blithering idiot! Not there . . . . further along the road. Bloody hell, this lot were at the end of the queue when brains were issued,' he ranted on as his unfortunate driver tried to get off to the side of the west-going dual carriageway. 'David, can you see if the SUV with that woman is behind us,' he continued, addressing his query to David Crawford-Slade.

'No, I can't,' he replied not even bothering to turn to look, 'and I say again that I see no point in us getting involved in this handover in Peshawar.'

'Well I suggest that you very quickly start to see the reason for us getting involved unless you are keen to spend the the rest of your life in prison. Once we've handed over the Pankhurst woman it's time to implement plan B which is when both you and I together disappear with our share of the heroin.'

'Do you really believe that, Hamish?' the Counsellor asked. 'That cretin Whistler will have spilled his guts under interrogation by the ISI. The only thing Gunn won't know is where we're meeting Mubashar and he'll be a long way behind us with all this traffic.'

'He'll fly to Peshawar with Gunn and Javed.'
'In what?'
'The ISI helicopter.'
'Bugger! I'd forgotten that. So he could be in Peshawar waiting for us.'
'Indeed.'
Their dialogue was interrupted by the radio.
'Brigadier Sahib, this is Mahood in SUV three, over.'
'Roger Mahood, yes, what is it? over'
'We are now by side of road. Imran and Shafiq both very dead. Bullet through head—both of them. What to do now Sahib? . . . . over.'

'Christ all bloody mighty! Only that bunch of fucking idiots could have screwed up the simplest of tasks of transporting that fucking woman from A to B,' Brigadier McCulloch swore, getting puce in the face and sweating profusely.'

'What's happened?' Crawford-Slade asked, who had not heard all of the transmission from the third SUV.

'What's happened? You ask David, just a minor hiccough in our plan. That fucking woman has somehow managed to kill both the driver and guard in her car and presumably is now driving back to Islamabad. That's what's happened.'

'But she hasn't overtaken us and she couldn't have got over the central reservation barriers so there can be only two options; she's either still behind us or she's taken the right fork to Mardan. Shafiq had the woman's handbag and cellphone, so she will be able to contact Gunn. General Kumari will know from his agents in Peshawar that Mubashar ali Munda is heading for Afghanistan via Chitral and the Dorah Pass. He will have passed that information on to Gunn who will arrange an RV with the Pankhurst woman. May I suggest that you instruct Mahood to catch up with us asap to see if that SUV is behind us and if not I suggest we go off-road, now that we've missed the turning, until we find the highway to Mardan. Make sense?'

SHOOT

'Yes I suppose so,' was admitted reluctantly by the Defence Attaché who then gave instructions to the third SUV to join them where they had pulled over on the side of the road.

*

From 20,000 feet above the Tribal Areas, Predator MQ1A's high-resolution cameras scanned the road that led north from Bannu over the Kohat Pass to Peshawar. Control of the RPV had been passed from its handlers at the launch site on an air strip in a secluded valley south of Sherobod in Uzbekistan to Langley via an encoded military satellite link. The Predator was armed with two Hellfire missiles and had now been airborne for eight hours, well short of even half its endurance capability of 22 hours. Today's target was the self-styled leader of the Pakistan Taliban, Mubashar ali Munda and his deputy Waheed Ahmed Rahim. Intreps from CIA agents operating in the Tribal Areas on the border with Pakistan indicated that the two men were heading for a meeting in Peshawar.

Below the Predator, two Suzuki 4x4's had just started to climb the twisting road that would take them over the Kohat Pass, some 35 miles to the south of Peshawar. Ten miles further south on the same road, a dilapidated and rusty Bedford truck with faded paint decoration, which had seen its best time fifty years earlier, also made its way to the pass.

'Zoom in on the registration plates of those two jeeps,' was ordered by the CIA officer commanding the mission. He had a remote VDU which copied that of the Predator handler.

'Roger to that, sir . . . . there,' and now on the screen was a view from the rear of the two jeeps as they negotiated the twisting hairpin bends of the Kohat Pass. 'Those are the plates we recorded when the target entered the vehicles in Bannu, sir.'

'Thank you Sergeant Roberts,' and the CIA officer pressed a button on his telephone. 'We have a positive ID of the target, sir.'

'Execute!'

'Roger that, sir . . . . execute Sergeant Roberts.'

'Roger sir . . . . missile away!' and twenty seconds later, 'target destroyed, sir.'

*

'The woman's escaped.'
'How?'
'She managed to kill both her guard and the driver.'
'So where is she now?'
'She has the car and we believe she's heading north in the direction of Swat.'
'And you, what are you doing?'
'Still heading for Peshawar and the handover of the merchandise.'
'Forget that—it'll take care of itself. Find that woman. Do I make myself clear?'
'Yes,' and the cellphone in the south of England ended the call which had been recorded by GCHQ in Cheltenham.

*

'That's one of the main junctions on the Grand Trunk Road you can see down there. One road continues to Peshawar and the other goes north to Swat and the mountains of the Hindu Kush . . . .'
'Sorry to interrupt you again, Javed, but the situation has changed in the last few minutes . . . . hold on, there's more news,' General Kumari held his hand up while he listened to another transmission. 'There's been an American drone strike to the south of Peshawar within the last half hour. The target was Mubashar ali Munda and his deputy. There's very little left of the the two cars, but they have been able to identify the severely burned body of Mubashar's deputy, Waheed. There's no sign of Mubashar. There are riots breaking out in every part of Peshawar, but worst of all in the bazaar . . . . wait, there's more. The police on the Grand Trunk Road have found two men on the side of the road . . . . both shot

through the head. A reluctant witness who was watering his goats by the side of the highway swears that the men were shot by a woman in Western clothing who dragged the bodies to the side of the road and then drove off in the car . . . . I think Ms Pankhurst has proved more than a match for her abductors,' was how the General finished his commentary on the rapidly unfolding events below them.

'I think we ought . . . .' but whatever Javed was thinking was interrupted by Gunn who was reading a text which he had just received on his secure cellphone.

'Wait a moment Javed as this text may help us decide what to do next. This is an intercept by GCHQ only ten minutes ago and now forwarded to me by BID and reads as follows: *"Telecon from a callbox in the South of England—from a different location to previous intercept—to cellphone in north west Pakistan. Woman has escaped and killed both driver and guard. Woman now in car and believed to be heading north on road to Swat. Forget your mission in Peshawar and find that woman."*

'That has to mean that she has taken that right fork in the road which we have just flown over . . . . either that or she could have headed back to Islamabad,' Javed added.

*

After a short diversion off-road, the two SUVs joined the northern highway to Mardan and pulled into the first filling station they came to. While Farooq and Jameel supervised the fuelling of the two SUVs, McCulloch and Crawford-Slade walked over to the coffee shop. Both men were wearing slacks and open-necked shirts; this form of dress and pale complexions attracted a number of unfriendly glances from the clientele in the shop. The news of the Predator strike had spread swiftly and the television in the filling station shop was carrying a newscast about the event and the riots in Peshawar.

'Holy shit! That's all we needed,' the DA muttered to Crawford-Slade. 'We'll be lucky not to get lynched in this part of the

Provence where the Taliban has many sympathisers. It's more important than ever that we head north to the Dorah Pass to meet up with Mubashar and hand over the Pankhurst woman as his bargaining tool. I'm just going to check with the guy at the till to find out if they've seen the other SUV and that woman.'

'OK, but don't let's hang about here because I'm beginning to feel very uncomfortable,' Crawford-Slade replied as he finished his coffee.

*

The road ahead of Emma stretched straight as an arrow across the flat agricultural plain between the east/west trunk road and the bleak foothills of the North West Frontier Provence and the gorges through which the Panjkora and Swat Rivers flowed. On either side of the road were Juniper and Aspen trees, all with their leaves shed as they prepared for the bitingly cold weather that would grip the foothills of the Hindu Kush within the next few weeks. She passed a sign for a filling station which drew her attention to the fuel gauge. 'Better fill up while I can and use the halt to see if my cellphone can reach anyone,' were her thoughts as she turned off the highway into the filling station. To her surprise, nothing in her handbag had been removed. At the back of the filling station buildings was an assortment of makeshift stalls selling everything from children's toys to jewellery and clothes. Once the car was full, Emma drove round to the parking lot at the back of the filling station and walked over to inspect the stalls.

In less than five minutes she had bought a complete outfit of traditional style female clothing which she took to the toilets and exchanged for her creased and blood-stained western clothing. Once that was done she took the cellphone out of her bag and checked the battery level. The level indicator showed that there was more than two-thirds power remaining and the cellphone showed a full three bars of signal strength. She still had Gunn's cellphone number so without much hope of success she quickly typed a text message and sent it:

"I've escaped from the DA and that other man from the BHC and am now at a filling station on the highway 10 miles south of Mardan."

*

'Wait! There's another text,' Gunn alerted Javed and General Kumari. 'It's from Emma. She's at a filling station on the highway about ten miles south of Mardan. Hang on guys I'll just let her know that we've received her text. I wonder how the hell she got hold of her cellphone,' Gunn muttered as he acknowledged the text. The General gave instructions to the pilot and the Alouette banked to the right as it turned to follow the northern highway. In just over five minutes the filling station was identified and the pilot brought the Alouette down onto the hard-baked ground just fifty yards short of the filling station. Gunn, Javed and the General got out of the helicopter and walked to the filling station where an emotional and overjoyed Emma met them.

'We've heard some fearsome accounts of your escape Miss Pankhurst,' the General teased her after being introduced and then continued by addressing all three of them. 'I must get back to Peshawar, my friends, as the demonstrations have developed into a major riot. My agents in that city tell me that Mubashar was well clear of the drone strike that killed his deputy. He's far too canny to offer such a tempting double target to the drone handlers. I have been told that Mubashar has bye-passed Peshawar and is heading north to Chitral and possibly the Dorah Pass into Afghanistan. If he has the nuclear warheads, perhaps he intends to hand them over to the Afghanistan Taliban or Al Qaeda. Should you decide you want to follow up on that intelligence report, please take this map,' and the General handed over the map which he had been studying throughout the helicopter flight from Islamabad. They said their farewells and the ISI General walked back to his helicopter.

'Let's sit down over a cup of coffee and make a decision on what to do next,' Gunn suggested as he led the way into the coffee shop adjacent to the filling station.

When they had been served with the pungent coffee and had listened to Emma's account of both her kidnap and escape, Gunn summed up their situation.

'We know that McCulloch and Crawford-Slade are heading this way looking for Emma. We have no idea whether they are ahead of us or behind us. The former would be my guess. We also know that Mubashar is heading in this direction on his way to a meeting with the Taliban to hand over the nuclear warheads. Stopping that transaction was the reason for the President's request for BID's assistance. That is what I get paid for and you receive your annual retainer, Javed,' Gunn added with a smile, but was interrupted by Emma.

'If you are about to say that searching for the nuclear warheads has nothing to do with me and . . . .'

'Woa . . . . woa, I was going to do nothing of the sort. Now that we know we have such a fearsome killer on our team I was going to suggest that we continue from this point as a threesome. Javed, we need your language skills, but does it make sense to follow up on the intelligence we've just been given by Rashid.'

'It's the only lead we have as to the possible location of the warheads. Our first and most important task was to find Emma—completed successfully largely through her efforts—so I agree . . . . continue. What about you?' Javed asked turning to Emma.

'For years I've been suffocated by the artificial life of business marketing which, I admit, has its excitement on occasions and has allowed me to live a pretty comfortable life, if perhaps somewhat dull. The most exciting things that have happened to me in my life have all occurred in the last ten days and so I'm all for continuing the search for the warheads and those bastards who kidnapped me.'

'Good, that's settled. I believe that the first thing to do is to get rid of the Toyota, which I suggest that we exchange for the best four-wheel-drive we can find in the used car lot at the back of this filling station. Then I intend to buy some traditional clothing with Javed's advice so that we blend in a little better into the local population. After that and a quick study of the map which Rashid gave us, I would like to head for the town of Dir at the junction of the Indus and Panjkora Rivers as our stop for tonight on our way to Chitral and the Dorah Pass; any questions?' There were none. 'Right, Javed can I leave the car exchange to you while I follow Emma's example by changing my clothes.'

Just under an hour later they were the third owner of a Chrysler Jeep with a full tank of diesel and two spare jerrycans of fuel. The Toyota SUV had been readily accepted in exchange for the Jeep and after a careful inspection and trial drive, Javed announced that it would serve them well with it's high and low ratio transfer gearbox on the unsurfaced, rugged mountain roads over the passes into the Chitral valley and on to Afghanistan over the Dorah Pass.

As Gunn and Emma were loading the jeep with various snacks and bottles of water, Javed joined them with information which he had gleaned by chatting to the man at the till.

'The man at the till told me that we are the second group of Europeans—his description, not mine—to have stopped by this station. He confirmed that there were two Toyotas, two Europeans and three Pakistanis. He said they left here about twenty minutes ago.'

'Right let's go. It'll be dark in a couple of hours and I would like to be clear of the Malakand Pass before then if possible,' Gunn said, climbing into the driving seat of the Jeep.

*

Ten miles ahead of them, the two Toyota SUVs came to the end of the highway and joined the rough, partially unsurfaced switchback road over the Malakand Pass.

CHAPTER 18

The SUV's had only driven half way up the switchbacks of the Malakand Pass when they came to a halt behind a queue of vehicles. McCulloch got out of the Toyota and walked up the line of cars, lorries and buses looking for the third SUV and Emma Pankhurst. After a hundred yards he came to the head of the queue to find a grossly over-laden lorry with broken rear leaf springs completely blocking the road. No one had gone up or down the pass for the last hour he was told by the third car driver he questioned who could speak English. He returned to Crawford-Slade.

'It'll be at least another half hour before they remove or repair the lorry that's blocking the road. Nothing has gone up or down the pass in the last hour. That confirms our belief that the woman has to be behind us. The worst case scenario is that Gunn and Iqbal have joined up with the Pankhurst woman and are on the road behind us also heading for Chitral to prevent Mubashar ali Munda from handing over the two warheads to Ahmad ali Ghazi of the Afghan Taliban. To earn our reward of £10 million of heroin, our task was to kidnap the woman and hand her over to Ahmad to use as a bargaining tool to prevent a SEAL or Predator operation to retrieve her and/or the warheads. To date we have signally failed in our task as the woman has escaped. I suggest that we deal with that trio right here on the pass. There's a sheer drop off the outer side of the road of over a thousand feet down to the Swat River in the valley below. No traffic is going to come down the pass so if we found a suitable ambush point, of which there must be many, we can recapture the woman and dispense with Gunn and Iqbal as a job lot. How's about that, David?' McCulloch asked Crawford-Slade.

'Only one snag that I can see, Hamish.'

'What's that?'

'It'll be dark in less than two hours, so how do we identify the car and the people in it?'

'They'll be less than an hour behind us, but if not we'll position Mahood or Farooq with one of our radios further down the road to identify the vehicle and warn us.'

'OK,' Crawford-Slade agreed with little conviction as they set off back down the pass to find a suitable ambush site.

*

The dual-carriageway finished at the town of Dargai and from then on the two-way road started to climb towards the pass. The higher they climbed the worse the road surface became until the tarmac disappeared completely. The sinking sun on their left as they drove north to the pass turned the snow from white to pink on the peaks of the Hind Kush.

'Think we'll be lucky to make Dir for our night stop; any suggestions, Javed?' Gunn asked as he engaged four wheel drive to get a better grip on the loose gravel of the road.

'Both Batkhela and Chakdarra are possibilities and at this time of year, most guest houses and hotels are only too glad of any occupancy. We certainly won't make Dir before nightfall. Chakdarra would be our best bet. Batkhela's only claim to fame is its bazaar which has the reputation of being the longest one in Pakistan. There's a Opal Oriental Hotel in Chakdarra which I've stayed in and survived, so perhaps that would be our best bet.'

'OK, on your head be it,' Gunn laughed and then added, 'but I think we may have to deal with Messrs McCulloch and Crawford-Slade before any night stop.'

They continued up the steep switchbacks of the pass with the road condition deteriorating rapidly amid clear signs of past rock-falls and landslides. There was no traffic coming in the opposite direction, but it was Emma who remarked on it.

'Ever since we reached the foot of this pass, we haven't seen a single vehicle coming down it in the opposite direction. Is that my imagination or could there be a reason for it.'

'You're quite right,' Javed agreed. 'Something has happened higher up the pass. It's a frequent occurrence. It'll be either a bus or lorry which has broken down and blocked the road. It means that we might have to turn round if it's a serious accident as I'm sure that we don't want to spend the night on this pass.'

'I can't say I fancy doing a 'U' turn on this road either if that's the alternative, but I suppose that's better than staying up here all night. It means that if McCulloch and his gang are ahead of us they could also be stuck,' Emma said and then added, 'look! there's a man on the side of the road ahead of us. Would it be worth asking him, Javed, if the road is blocked?'

'Why not . . . . if you pull over John, I'll ask . . . . no cancel that . . . . that's a radio he's holding. Emma! Duck right down so he can't see you.' The urgency in Javed's voice made Emma react immediately and she lay down across the back seat of the Jeep, but it was a close call if she had been quicker enough. They drove past the man who stared at the Jeep's occupants. Once they were past him he raised the small hand-held radio and spoke into it. 'He's speaking into the radio, but we won't know whether we fooled him with the change of vehicle. Once we're out of sight round the next hairpin, pull in as close to the inside rock-face as you can and I'll go back to see what he's up to.'

Once they had driven round the next rock buttress, Gunn pulled in to the side as close to the crumbling rock face as possible. Javed jumped out before the nearside door was pinned against the rock face, unsheathing a razor sharp knife as he left the Jeep. The light was now fading fast and even if the blockage in the road ahead of them was cleared in the next few minutes, there was no question of them being able to get any further than Chakdarra on the Swat River.

'That knife which Javed produced suddenly turned him from a charming tourist guide and friend into a frightening brigand,' Emma confided as she and Gunn waited for Javed's return.

'My first visit to this Country, but the briefing I was given back at the 'House' covered his background. His father commanded one of the most famous Indian regiments which fought with quite extraordinary courage against the Japanese in the Second World War. He has been bred from a family of warriors so he more than knows how to look after himself,' Gunn added.

'Which house is that?'

'Sorry, it's a term that's used for Kingsroad House, the head office of BID in London.' They heard nothing of Javed's return until he opened the offside rear door.

'No more problems from that source. I managed to get quite close to him and could hear what he was saying on the radio. I'm afraid I wasn't quick enough, Emma, he was telling the DA that a Jeep had just passed with two men and a woman and no sign of the Toyota. The other three will be waiting up ahead of us.'

'What do you think that man will do now?' Emma asked.

'Not much unless he's able to fly. He's somewhere down in the Swat River below us. John, shall I take the wheel for a bit and leave you free to handle the weapons. Here's the man's radio,' and Javed handed over the small hand-held radio to Gunn.

'Sounds good,' and the two men swapped places. Emma was silent. The cold-blooded killing of the sentry posted to watch out for them shocked her, even though they were the men who had kidnapped her. She had told Gunn that she wanted to be a part of mission so there was no point in being squeamish now, she reasoned, as the Jeep pulled out from the inside rock face of the pass and continued up the rough track.

The Jeep had only gone a few hundred yards when the radio burst into life.

'Hello Mahood, this is Brigadier Sahib, are there any more cars coming up the pass?'

Gunn handed the radio to Javed who gave a very convincing linguistic reply.

'Sahib, this is Mahood,' followed by a muttered Urdu curse, 'only one car, Brigadier Sahib, this car is coming to you very soon, over.'

'Roger Mahood, stay where you are, out.' Javed handed the radio back to Gunn.

'All ready to deal with this lot?' Javed checked.

'Here Emma,' and Gunn handed the small Glock 26 to her. 'No safety catch, just point and pull the trigger. I'll leave the AK47 for you, Javed. OK Javed, let's get on with it.'

As the Jeep rounded the next hairpin one of the two Toyotas pulled out from the side of the road and with headlights on high beam drove directly at the Jeep with the clear intention of forcing it into the void over the side of the road. The Toyota struck the Jeep on the nearside with tremendous force, crumpling the bodywork against the wheel and forcing the Jeep back to the outer edge of the road. The Jeep's rear wheels went over the side and it seemed that it was about to go over, but the four wheel drive to the front wheels gripped the gravel surface of the road and the Jeep slewed back onto the road. The Toyota made another charge at the Jeep, gravel spitting from its racing rear wheels. Gunn and Javed could see the faces of McCulloch and Crawford-Slade distorted with malicious grins as they prepared to push the Jeep over the edge into the abyss below. At the very last second when Emma thought that it was all over, Javed twisted the wheel and gunned the engine. The Jeep executed a half-doughnut, spinning in a semi circle and, like a sprinting rugby player jinking to avoid a tackle, side-stepped the head-on charge of the Toyota. With nothing to halt its impetus the Toyota kept on going, straight over the edge of the road, the screams of its two occupants echoing back off the rock face.

Javed pulled the Jeep into the side of the road by the other Toyota. Of the two Pakistanis there was no sign. Gunn walked over to the Toyota and looked inside. 'Ignition key's still here,' he told the other two. 'Why don't we get rid of the Jeep as its nearside wheel is a right-off and replace it with this.'

'Good idea,' Javed agreed and they transferred their bits and pieces from the Jeep to the Toyota. This included switching the number plates as the Toyota still had its diplomatic plates. Javed climbed back into the Jeep, started it and drove it at the edge of the road, let in the clutch and jumped clear. The Jeep disappeared over the side of the road. 'I think we'll just leave that for the Pakistani Police to solve when the two vehicles are found.'

'What about the other two Pakistanis who were with them?' Emma asked.

'No one will see hair or hide of those two, Emma. They'll return to their families, wherever that may be and I very much doubt that they'll come anywhere near the the British High Commission in Islamabad.'

'OK, jump in you two,' Gunn encouraged, 'and let's see if they've managed to unblock the road, so we can get to Chakdarra and some form of bed for the night. That's the end of a very long and eventful day's introduction to Pakistan for me and I'm ready for bed.' There was no disagreement from the other two.

There was one lane clear when they reached the broken down lorry. After waiting their turn to squeeze past the lorry unnervingly close to the outside of the road, they continued over the pass and finally reached Chakdarra shortly before 9 pm that evening.

*

Something or some noise had awoken Gunn from a deep sleep. He lay still while he gathered his senses. The Opal Oriental bedroom was in total darkness—with not even a trace of ambient light seeping into the bedroom from the edge of the curtains. The hotel reception the previous evening had been delighted to sell three of its double bedrooms during an out-of-season period and after a very simple meal the three of them had retired to bed, but not before Emma had paid a visit to the hotel shop which had to be opened especially for her. Gunn glanced at the luminous hands of his watch . . . . 2.15 . . . . they had agreed to rise at six in the morning for an early start . . . . four hours more of sleep . . . . and then he was wide awake as his eyes, now accustomed to the dark, identified a person standing beside his bed.

That realisation was quickly followed by the now familiar aroma of a perfume he had become used to since the night in the Plaza Hotel in Milton Keynes when Emma and he had made love for the first time. Gunn sat up and swung his legs out of the bed. Emma was completely naked and moved towards him so that the silky soft hair of her groin brushed against his mouth. She moaned with delight as his tongue found her erect clitoris and she pressed him closer to her groin. He lifted her onto the bed where she straddled him and pushed his erect penis deep inside her. After a day full of action one moment and terrifying fear another, both of them reached their orgasms almost instantly and lay, momentarily exhausted, in each other's arms. They made love again more slowly and then both drifted into a deep sleep before the first grey light of dawn filtered round the edge of the curtains.

CHAPTER 19

'Why's that red light flashing?' Emma asked as Gunn fitted a short stubby aerial to the top of his cellphone.

'It's telling me to convert this cellphone into a satellite phone so that BID can send an encrypted message to me,' Gunn explained as he delved in his backpack for various bits and pieces.

'Did you have that aerial fitted when I texted you from that petrol station?'

'No . . . . no need; the cellphone works well off the cell-aerial network in this country, but in remote areas you'll be lucky to get any signal at all. I was up in the General's helicopter where this phone picked up your text with no problem. With this aerial, the transmission goes direct to a communications satellite somewhere up above us and any encrypted message is impossible to block or hack.'

'Do you want that gun you gave me yesterday?'

'No, you hang on to it . . . . in fact it might be a good idea for you to take a few practice shots as it's completely deserted around here at the moment. Oh, that reminds me of something I have been meaning to ask you since our early start this morning.'

'What was that?'

'How did you manage to get into my room last night?'

'Ah hah! that's my secret,' and Emma went back to the Toyota where Javed had produced a thermos of coffee.

The trio had set off from the hotel shortly after 6.3am and an hour and a half later were driving through the almost deserted town of Timargarha when Gunn's cellphone alerted him of an incoming encrypted text which required him to fit the satellite aerial to the phone. They had pulled off to the side of the road close to the Panjkora River.

> "Intrep as at 0100211020912. This rep acks your telecon via ISI Islamabad that you now have British female. Presume two BHC British males responsible for kidnap of female are now neutralised. Pse confirm. Sigint from GCHQ and Humint sourced from CIA. Target is in 1950s-era Bedford lorry covered in painted scenes from the Koran. There are two lorries which are identical in appearance. Humint confirms that Dorah Pass will be the crossing point into Afghanistan after a halt at Garam Chasma to on-load weapons, explosives and pick up an armed escort of Taliban. Humint has confirmed that the two nuclear warheads are on one of the lorries. No indication of which one. Lorries last identified by Predator approaching the Lowari Pass. CIA Humint is in one of the lorries so Predator was unable to strike. Your mission now to identify which lorry is carrying the warheads so that lorry and target can be destroyed by Predator strike. Using this means will produce a Predator overhead within three minutes for the next 48 hours. You should be aware that Mubashar ali Munda knows of your presence in the area as he had hoped to have the British female as a hostage to prevent Predator strikes. Ack this comm."

Gunn acknowledged the transmission, confirmed that McCulloch and Crawford-Slade were dead and requested advice on identifying the CIA agent with the Taliban escorting Mubashar. There was a pause of about 30 seconds after he transmitted his report and then just three words were sent in reply:

"You know him."

He walked over to join the other two at the SUV. Javed poured some coffee into the thermos lid and handed it to Gunn.

'Any change of plan?'

'No not really; Mubashar is about sixty miles ahead of us on the Lowari Pass . . . . destination the Dorah Pass into Afghanistan via Garam Chasma to load up with more weapons and more Taliban. He's in one of two lorries covered in painted scenes from the Koran. My task is to identify that lorry so that a Predator can obliterate it with a Hellfire missile strike. Only problem is that the CIA have an undercover agent travelling with Mubashar. That agent is Doyle Barnes; I've known him ever since we were both in our respective armies. We both trained together at Fort Bragg when he was with 82nd Airborne Division and I was in the Parachute Brigade. He's a fluent Arabic and Pashtu speaker and a very high value CIA asset because his presence has prevented a Predator strike up until now. So for now we press on to catch up with the lorries. CIA has a Predator constantly airborne over this area for the next 48 hours. Emma, grab that automatic and we'll give you a chance to get used to it. I reckon that we'll probably need all the firepower we can muster if we are to succeed in this mission.'

Emma was surprised with the accuracy she was able to achieve after only five or six rounds fired at a pile of stones some twenty yards away. When she had fired all 8 rounds in the magazine they returned to the Toyota, finished the coffee and set off again. The road was surfaced, but it would have been preferable were it not so as the frosts and ice of previous winters had destroyed the tarmac and left deep potholes which were more than capable of snapping an axle as easily as a chicken bone. Gunn was driving and they made as best speed as possible; the only consolation was the hope that the Bedford lorry would be making much slower progress. In just short of two hours they arrived at the foot of the Lowari Pass which rose to a height of 3,200 metres before descending into the spectacular Chitral valley. Here the tarmac surface disappeared and the road over the pass was rock and gravel hewn out of the mountain.

On three occasions they met buses coming down the pass in the opposite direction. Fortunately, as Pakistan, like India, drives on the left—when not driving in the middle of the road—Gunn was able to hug the inside of the road while the buses swerved with casual disdain, driver holding the wheel with one hand while lighting a cigarette with the other, to the outside of the treacherous track, often with half a tyre's width over the side of the precipitous abyss. Emma decided that the best way to overcome these encounters was to shut her eyes. It took them just under an hour to reach the col at the top of the pass. The panoramic view down into Chitral, with the early morning sun lighting the snows on the peak of the 8,000 metre Tirich Mir at the northern head of the valley, took Emma's breath away.

'Please stop, just for a minute, John, while I take a photo. That view's just like the description of 'Shangri La' in James Hilton's Lost Horizon . . . . one of my favourite books,' Emma added as she climbed out of the Toyota and took several photos with her cell-phone.

'I had no idea that this northern part of Pakistan was so luxuriant with its scenery. That view is simply stunning,' Gunn added to Emma's enjoyment of the view.

'I was hoping that might be your reaction,' Javed smiled, at their enjoyment of the scenery. 'There're many more places that are just as scenic. You must come back and drive up the the Karakorum Highway to see Nunga Parbat, the mountain that overshadows the Fairytale Meadow, and marvel at the tent-pegging and polo skills of the horsemen in Gilgit.'

'Thanks, I couldn't resist that photo,' a slightly breathless Emma said as she returned to the car. 'What height are we at?' she asked as Gunn set off once again.

'Just over 10,000feet,' Javed supplied the answer, 'and now I'm afraid that we have to take the outside of the track down the pass.'

They had only been driving for five minutes when something caught Javed's attention further down the pass. He asked Gunn if he had any binoculars amongst all the other 'bits and pieces' in his back-pack.

'Sure,' Gunn replied. 'Emma can you delve in the pack and dig out the binos.'

Emma handed the binoculars to Javed who adjusted the focus for his eyesight and then studied an area of the pass well below them.

'Thought so,' Javed muttered.

'Problem?' Gunn asked

'No, I'm almost certain that we've caught up with the Mubashar convoy. Neither of us has shaved, which will help to make us less noticeable, but we ought to have bought a burka for Emma.'

'No problem guys,' and Emma produced a black burka from a Plaza Hotel plastic bag. 'I bought two of these last night at the hotel shop.'

*

Doyle Barnes tried again to get a more comfortable position on the slatted wooden bench seat in the back of the lorry as his backside was going numb. There were twenty-one other volunteer freedom fighters like him squashed into the back of the ancient Bedford lorry. Most of them were Pakistanis, schooled and brainwashed in the radicalised Madrassas of the North West Frontier Provence and Waziristan, but a handful came from other countries. He had singled out a pair of British Muslim converts who had told him they came from Bradford, another one was from New York and the rest were a mixture of Egyptians, Syrians and Palestinians from the Gaza Strip. They were watched closely by four Afghan Taliban fighters. Somewhere behind them and at a distance that would make it impossible for a drone to get both vehicles in one strike was the other lorry, carrying the leader of the Pakistan Taliban, the warheads and—as yet undeclared by the USA—the US Ambassador to Islamabad who had been kidnapped the day before at the opening ceremony of the trade expo in Islamabad.

Doyle's shock of black hair, high cheekbones and deeply tanned complexion, together with his fluent Pashtu and Arabic supported his alias as Raza Ayub Khan, a Pathan from the weapon-making town of Darra. The fearsome reputation of the Pathan *pukhtunwali* or 'way of the Pathans'—a law which ignores the governance of Pakistan—meant that the rest of his fellow freedom fighters steered well clear of him. The CIA had infiltrated Doyle into a remote Taliban training camp in Waziristan. He and all his fellow recruits had been thoroughly searched, so there was no possibility of hiding a cellphone or contacting anyone to pass on information about the location of the warheads or to get help with rescuing Charles Darmody, the US Ambassador. Besides all those problems he had a far more imminent problem which was the need to urinate. He raised his arm and immediately an AK47 swung round to cover him.

'I need to relieve myself, efendi.' It was stated as a fact. No Pathan would ask for permission to relieve himself. Several others muttered their wish to relieve themselves. The AK47 swung away and the Taliban guard spoke into a radio. He then banged on the small window in the back of the driving cab and the lorry pulled over to the side of the road. The guards let down the lorry's tailgate and jumped down. They then told the volunteer fighters to jump down and line up on the nearside of the lorry and urinate. No privacy was given and none expected.

*

Gunn's cellphone alerted him to accept another encrypted transmission. He pulled over into a wider part of the road used for passing vehicles and pressed the receive button on the phone.

> *"BID from Director for Gunn. CIA has informed us that the US Ambassador, Mr Charles Darmody, was kidnapped at the trade fair yesterday and is travelling as a hostage with Mubashar ali Munda and the warheads. This makes a drone strike even more risky. Please advise when and if you have a plan. Ack."*

Gunn acknowledged the transmission and pulled out onto the road again. No vehicle had passed them in either direction while he had read and acknowledged the BID message. Twice more as they weaved their way down the pass, Gunn had to inch out to the outer edge of the road to allow a lorry the first time and then a bus the second time, stacked with bags, humans, goats and chicken on the roof. Javed believed that he had spotted the two lorries but they were two far away for a positive identification.

'Do you think they'll stop in Chitral or continue on to Garam . . . . whatever?' Emma asked.

'My guess would be the latter . . . . Garam Chasma . . . . the name means 'hot springs' and it does have plenty of them where you can take a bath in the hot sulphurous water,' Javed replied.

'Oooh, I'd love to treat myself to a hot bath right now,' Emma mused allowed.

'There's no privacy for the bathers and the appearance of a pretty Caucasian woman in the baths would cause a riot. This is a fiercely radical Muslim area so please don't be tempted. The town is well known as a Taliban hotbed. I think it has a couple of hotels and a national tourist hostel, but many of the Taliban either sleep in the open or in tents spending many hours at night sitting round open fires smoking hash. No police come anywhere nearer than Chitral or drive straight through, usually in a convoy of no less than two or more vehicles.'

'Thanks for the warning, Javed. Any ideas for a plan of action, John?' Emma turned to Gunn.

'Not much at the moment, to be honest. Our first task is to find where they've stopped for the night—that is, if they do stop. They could easily drive on into Afghanistan. If they do stop then we need to approach Garam Chasma for a recce and, if possible, find the warheads and my CIA buddy, Doyle Barnes; Javed, your advice?'

'We're all wearing traditional style clothing so I can be a tourist guide speaking in a mixture of Pashtu and Arabic and you, John, use your Arabic. You wouldn't be expected to contribute to the conversation, Emma, except to whisper to your 'husband', so that would be my advice and, like John, I suggest we drive on to Garam Chasma and ostensibly look for hotel accommodation at the same time as looking for Mubashar's lorries.'

It took them another two hours to reach Chitral where the surfaced road stopped and only rough gravelled roads continued to

Kosht in the north and Garam Chasma and the the Dorah Pass to the west. They were rewarded with a spectacular view of the Chitral valley as they approached the town, with its white mosque on the edge of a vivid blue lake surrounded by lush fields and trees. The view brought gasps of appreciation from Emma.

'I had no idea that there were such beautiful places in this part of Pakistan. I've always thought that this whole area was just dust, scrub and rock. Do many tourists visit this part of your Country?' she asked Javed.

'In the days of the Raj this whole area was the centre of the trekking habit of the British which is when the hotels and rest houses were built. Before the Gulf Wars and the spread of radical Islam, the tourist trade was developing well. That has virtually ceased as most governments warn their nationals to steer clear of this area. I understand that it's almost impossible to get travel insurance if this part of Pakistan is your destination.'

'Do we need to stop here, Javed?' Gunn asked as he drove into the main street of the town which wound its way through the bazaar.

'Pull over to that petrol station on the left and we can top up with diesel there and get something to eat as I'm feeling a bit peckish,' Javed suggested and then added after studying the map which they had been given by General Kumari, 'we continue on this road for about five or six miles after leaving the town. After we cross the river there's a left turn which takes us to Garam Chasma.'

'I'll second that Javed,' Emma said and then added, 'I could do real justice to a curry.'

'Let's see what Garam Chasma has to offer,' Gunn suggested, getting back into the Toyota after paying for the diesel and buying a bagful of hot crispy samosas from the store beside the petrol station.

CHAPTER 20

Now that they had reached 'bandit country' in the hills to the west of Chitral, the Afghan Taliban guards had rolled up the canvas curtain above the lorry's tailgate. At last Doyle Barnes was able to confirm that they were heading for the Dorah Pass into Afghanistan. The rough, potholed road zig-zagged up the steep gradient of the snow-covered peak of Tirich Mir until the ancient Bedford lorry ground its way into the village of Garam Chasma.

The lorry was quickly surrounded by the local inhabitants—the majority shouting and cheering their approval, but Doyle noticed that there were some who seemed less keen to see the new arrivals. The village clustered around the banks of the river which ran through it and the steaming pools fed by the hot springs. The lorry came to a halt and the guards told them to get off. It was early afternoon and there was still a little warmth in the sun, but once that had set the temperature would plummet. The only thing to protect Doyle against the cold was his locally spun 'choga' and a couple of blankets slung over his shoulder. Some of the new Taliban recruits had nothing except what they were wearing and would have to rely on getting as close to the fires which would be lit as dusk fell, if they were to survive.

The village lay in a hollow, scooped out of the harsh rocky surrounds through which the river ran and where the hot springs bubbled up into pools. There was only one main street through the village with bazaar stalls on either side. The houses, or dwelling shacks, rose in tiers up the steep sides of the mountain. Doyle and his fellow radicalised Taliban were led to an area where the houses were more substantial and where the other lorry was now parked; once again there was a distance of nearly 200 yards between the two lorries. In the open ground in front of the houses, the fires had already been lit and there were lean-to shelters and shacks where their guards indicated they should put their bedding—if they had brought any. The new recruits were told that a meal would be provided and they could wander round the village if they so wished. Even as they were being told this, large cooking pots were brought out from the main house and placed on the fires.

Doyle decided to walk into the village to test the reaction of the Taliban. Others joined him, but the guards appeared not to be too worried and the reason for their lack of concern became obvious when Doyle realised that the entire village was populated by the Taliban, all of them armed with various weapons. 'No wonder the police never come here,' Doyle thought as he wandered from one stall to another. He and all of those who had come with him in the back of the lorry were watched closely. Any attempt to find a telephone or any other form of communication would be snuffed out instantly.

*

'Just pull over, John, and I'll ask some of these villagers if there is any accommodation,' Javed suggested as they reached Garam Chasma just as the sun was setting. After a lot of arm waving and pointing in various directions, Javed returned to the Toyota. 'There's a hotel Innjigaan just to the east of the bazaar which the villagers say is used by tourists. I was told the first right turn just along the main road through the bazaar will take us to the hotel.'

Gunn weaved the Toyota through the curious local inhabitants until he reached the right turn.

'Just as well we changed those registration plates,' Gunn commented as he spotted the hotel, on slightly higher ground above a number of steaming hot springs. There were screens around some of the pools which Javed explained were there to prevent voyeurs watching the women bathe.

'Please don't be tempted Emma,' Javed cautioned, 'as we'll have the whole village down here.'

'It's very tempting, but I'll just stay smelly!'

The hotel was basic and empty, but did have its own restaurant and now that it was dark, candles and hurricane lamps had been lit giving the interior a cosy atmosphere. Having selected their bedrooms in case they were fortunate enough to get any sleep, the three of them met on the terrace overlooking the pools and with a fading view of the the peak of Tirich Mir as the sun sank below the Hindu Kush.

'Time isn't on our side,' Gunn kicked off the discussion, and then continued, 'Mubashar may move on tonight and we can't afford to miss the opportunity—if one should present itself—of dealing with him tonight.'

'What about your CIA friend and the US Ambassador?' Javed queried.

'Not forgotten Javed; I suggest that we all three go into the village and with your help see if we can find where the lorries have been parked up for the night so that at least we know where our target is.'

'Agreed; we should stick together. Under that burka, Emma, you have the perfect disguise and Gunn's unshaven stubble makes him almost a local!'

The three of them walked the short distance into the village and then turned right heading for the higher ground as they had seen no sign of the lorries to the left, where they had entered Garam Chasma. It was the hour in the evening when all the shop fronts were lit—mostly by hurricane lamps, but the whirr of a generator in the background of some stalls and the addition of electric lighting lit up the narrow street through the bazaar. Everywhere they looked, they were surrounded by men armed with AK47s and curved bladed knives hanging from shoulder straps.

Emma had paused to admire some of the needlework in the locally spun cloth. Javed stayed close to her in case a question or remark was made to her by the shop owner. Gunn was covering their backs keeping an eye on anything and everything that moved . . . . and then he thought he must be hallucinating as he could hear someone whistling the unmistakeable tune of the US 82nd Airborne Marching Song, somewhere in the the throng of people moving to and fro in the street. He shook his head . . . . yes, there it was again. He looked at the sea of faces around him, most of them either expressionless, scowling or covered by burkas. It had stopped. 'Must've been my imagination,' he muttered to himself. Javed and Emma finished their inspection of the local cloth and joined him.

'You look as though you've seen a ghost!' Javed said in Arabic to Gunn.

'Shhhh! listen Javed.' And sure enough, the Marching Song of the 82nd Airborne was being whistled by someone. 'There's only one person within a thousand miles of us here who would whistle that and know that I would recognise it.'

'Your buddy in the CIA? Did he know that you were out here?'

'BID and the CIA do work very closely and he is the liaison agent from their side as I am from BID. So I would like to think that our joint selection for this task was planned and not just a coincidence. Follow me, but stay back a touch in case this is some sort of trap. OK?'

'Yes got it,' and Javed and Emma dropped back while Gunn moved forward through the crowd, straining his hearing to pick up the tune once again. The whistling had stopped. Gunn scanned the faces all around him, but none registered any recognition.

'Salaam alaikum!'

Gunn turned, to find his friend beside him who continued in Arabic.

'You recognised the marching song?'

'We sang it often enough on those forced marches.'

'Come with me and bring your friends. I've found a place where we can talk and plan. Who is under the burka? Another of your girlfriends, you crafty secret agent; you'll have to introduce me when we get to our safe house.'

'You have such a place?'

'Oh yes, very necessary since the SEAL op' against bin Laden.'

Gunn beckoned to Javed and Emma and, with Doyle, led the way to a shop selling every conceivable type of weapon, all made on the premises. Doyle led them down the side of the small shop and then stopped at a door on his left. Gunn didn't catch what was said, but the door opened and all four of them were welcomed in before the door was firmly closed by the stooped old man who had opened the door. They found themselves in a simple, but comfortable room lit by electric light.

'Please take a seat,' was said in English by their host who now stood erect from his stoop.

'Let me introduce Parvez Rathore, a.k.a Simon Brewer of the CIA,' Doyle said with a smile at the surprise the transformation had caused.

'Thank heavens! I can take off this burka,' Emma said with real feeling as she was introduced to their host. Once they were seated, Simon continued with his brief.

'We have very little time to rescue the Ambassador and destroy the warheads. Your timely arrival will be a great help. We knew that you were in the region, but did not know how close behind Mubashar ali Munda you were,' Simon explained as he poured scalding hot tea into cups and handed them around. 'It's now just after seven. At 9.30, I and some locally recruited helpers will create a disturbance in the area where the lorries are parked up. Doyle has already confirmed that Darmody is kept in the lorry with the warheads. Just behind that seat you're sitting on Emma is enough C4 explosive to turn the lorry and the warheads into scrap metal. While I and my recruits create the diversion, I would like Doyle and the three of you to rescue Darmody and place the bomb. It has a very short timing mechanism of three minutes which is long enough for you to put a survivable distance between the lorry and yourselves, but not long enough for anyone to tamper with the device. Tight timings I know, you guys, but lack of time prevents us from planning anything more sophisticated. Questions?'

'Yes Simon,' came from Emma. 'I'm not familiar with nuclear warheads so I assume that blowing up the two warheads in the lorry won't create another Hiroshima.'

'Thanks for that Emma. No, a nuclear device has to be detonated in a very specific way by compressing two sub-critical masses of weapon-grade uranium—or plutonium—together in a targeted detonation. In this case the two warheads will disintegrate with the explosion of the C4.'

'Phew! that's reassuring,' and they all laughed which eased the slight tension in the atmosphere.

'One more aspect of the explosive device I've made up for you to leave in the lorry. It will also transmit a signal to the drone which is cruising above us right now. The drone will react to the explosion of the device and initiate a Hellfire missile strike on the lorry location, so it's probably not necessary to tell you to get well clear. Lastly, there's one more part to this plan; there's a stealth modified Pave Hawk SAR helicopter on standby over the border which will lift all of you on the code word RAT-TRAP. It will home-in on the transmission of your satellite phone, John,' Simon concluded by addressing the point to Gunn.

'And what happens to you after this explosion and hopefully all of us get picked up by the helicopter?' Emma asked.

'Oh, not much; this village will return to its usual life of cultivating poppies for the heroin trade, selling weapons to the tribesmen and terrorists and I will do my best to keep Langley informed of what is happening in this stunningly scenic, but wild and evil part of the world. Most of these radicalised guys buy their weapons from me. The weapons they see in the shop are very different from the ones I sell to them. I make those out of very poor quality steel so they are likely to be as dangerous to the firer as the target. Right, come on everyone, time to get going. Oh, you might need these,' and he produced a pair of powerful bolt cutters before continuing, 'I suggest that you get your car up here. You can park it on the other side of the street about fifty yards in that direction,' Simon pointed, 'and then it will be ready for a rapid departure if you need it.'

They got up to leave and said their farewells; Emma was quite emotional and hugged the lone CIA agent before they left with Gunn carrying the IED constructed by Simon and the bolt cutters.

'I can't help feeling that we won't ever see him again,' she confided on the verge of tears to the three men with her.

'He's been doing this now for nearly ten years and when offered a change of location or job has always turned it down. He likes to be on his own. None of us has any idea about his background or if there is some reason for his preference for this life,' Doyle explained as they walked back to the hotel. 'Do you have silencers for your automatics?' Doyle asked as they reached the hotel. Both Gunn and Javed nodded. 'OK, back out here in five and then we'll drive to the parking slot in the main street and then I'll lead you to the target lorry. How we tackle the men guarding the lorry can only be decided when we get there. Are you armed Emma?'

'Yes, but my Glock isn't silenced.'

'Right, stay close, take cover when we do and use your automatic without hesitation if you have to—OK?'

'OK,' and with no further discussion they went into the hotel and reappeared a few minutes later.

Doyle led the way back along the street through the bazaar, until they branched off to the left leading to the flat area where the lorries were parked—one at either end of the open area. There were now a dozen or more cooking fires burning and the aroma of curried lamb drifted towards the group of four as they mingled with other Taliban—assuming, Emma thought—that those covered by burkas like her were women. Javed was carrying the AK47 as it seemed that it was the accoutrement of necessity for the well-dressed terrorist. Doyle stopped and without pointing indicated the lorry closest to them and the house which appeared to be the stopover for the hierarchy of this echelon of Taliban.

'That was the lorry with the bombs and Ambassador, but I'll check because they keep changing them around,' Doyle murmured and slipped away amongst the crowd of tribesmen.

It was now full dark and very little detail could be seen except the faces of the men squatting by the fires, wrapped in their chogas and blankets against the falling temperature. Doyle returned and told them that the lorries had been changed. Gunn checked his watch . . . . it was now 9.15. Just 15 minutes to go before Simon's disturbance. They stopped some 50 yards from the lorry. There were at least five or six men whom they could see, either guarding the lorry or making it very difficult to get near without raising an alarm. It was Emma who spotted the weak point. She dug Gunn in the side.

'Look! That's a woman in a burka going into the lorry carrying what looks like a cooking pot. If we could deal with her when she comes out and then I go back into the lorry it might be our only way of releasing the Ambassador.'

'She's right John, those steps have been placed at the tailgate of the lorry to make it easier for women to get into the lorry,' Javed supported Emma's suggestion.

'I can't think of any other way. Here, you take this,' and Gunn removed the silencer from his Glock and fitted it onto Emma's smaller automatic and gave her his torch and his small Swiss Army knife. 'You never know, he might be tied up with rope.' He then looked around and spotted an empty cooking pot behind a group of men which he picked up. 'Here, take this and follow the woman when she comes out. Use that,' and Gunn pointed to the Glock, 'however distasteful it may be. Just keep reminding yourself what they will do to you—and us, if we're caught.'

Holding the cooking pot in one hand with the Glock inside it and the bolt-cutters in the other concealed by the folds of her burka, Emma walked confidently towards the lorry. Gunn, Doyle and Javed edged closer with weapons all ready to provide covering fire if the guards were suspicious of Emma's intention.

The flap at the back of the lorry was lifted and the burka-clad woman appeared, gingerly coming down the steps because of the restricted vision afforded by the eye aperture in the burka. She reached the ground, turned to her right and walked towards a darker area beyond where the guards were standing. Emma followed her and almost immediately both disappeared into the darkness. There was no reaction from the men standing behind the lorry. Barely half a minute later the burka clad figure reappeared.

'Is that Emma?' Gunn whispered to Javed.

'No idea; how can you tell?'

The burka-clad figure climbed the steps into the back of the lorry and disappeared behind the canvas curtain. The minutes dragged by giving the three men no idea of what might be happening inside the lorry. What seemed like half-an-hour, but was less than five minutes, the burka reappeared and walked round to the side of the lorry where she could not be seen by the guards. The men edged slowly in her direction. One of the guards turned and saw Doyle whom he recognised and remembered to address him in Pashtu rather than Urdu.

'What's up with you, my friend?' was asked.

'Oh shit! that's it,' Gunn muttered to Javed as he grasped the butt of the Glock under his choga.

'No hang on, John . . . . wait . . . . Doyle's telling him that he suffers from a weak bladder and is just going for a pee behind the lorry.'

The guard had turned back to the group he was with by a warming fire and made some joke about Doyle's bladder problem which caused a ripple of laughter. The three of them made it to the far side of the lorry where they found the burka-clad figure of Emma.

'Both the bombs and the Ambassador are in there. It's very cold and although they have provided him with blankets and a bed of straw-filled sacks, I wouldn't be surprised if he was very close to suffering from hypothermia. Here's the torch and the silencer, John. Charles Darmody's got the knife and . . . .' even as Emma spoke the canvas side curtain of the lorry was cut in the shape of a window and all three men reached up and helped the Ambassador out of the lorry.

'No idea who you guys are, but thanks, I don't think I'd have survived the night in that freezing cold lorry,' was muttered through chattering teeth. Doyle immediately took one of the blankets that were slung over his shoulder and wrapped it around the Ambassador. 'They check on me about every ten minutes, so we'll need to get away pretty smartly.'

Doyle and Javed heaved Gunn up through the aperture in the side curtain and passed the IED and torch to him. That was the exact moment that two of the guards came round the back of the lorry and confronted them.

CHAPTER 21

Phhhht . . . . phhhht! The two silenced shots from Javed's automatic were fired so quickly that they almost sounded as just one shot. The two Taliban guards dropped silently to the ground.

'Quick! help me drag them out of sight,' but no exhortation from Javed was necessary as Doyle and Emma jumped into action to heave the two bodies away from the rear of the lorry. 'Get the clothes off this one,' Javed directed, as he started to pull the outer layer of clothing off the man. 'Sorry Ambassador, but we need to disguise you with some of this rather smelly clothing,' Javed added, as he approached Charles Darmody.

'No problem . . . . and please don't call me Ambassador. Most of my family and friends call me Chuck . . . . much quicker!'

'Right Chuck,' Javed said helping him to dress in the clothes and hat of one of the guards. As soon as that was complete, Doyle handed one of the AK47s to Chuck.

'I bet you've handled one of these before,' Doyle said and then added, 'oh we forgot to introduce ourselves . . . . that marksman with the automatic is Javed. Both he and the guy inside the lorry are from British Intelligence. Adding a touch of glamour to our team is Emma, head of marketing for Universal Switchgear and I'm Doyle from the CIA. That's about it.'

'A privilege to join your team. What happens now?'

'That rather depends on what John does in the back of the lorry.'

*

Right beside the pile of straw sacks on which the Ambassador had been placed with both hands and feet tied with plastic cable ties, were two large crates measuring some six feet in length and two feet in both other dimensions. The writing on the boxes was in Urdu script and so only partially intelligible to Gunn because of the similarity to Arabic script. They were the warheads for Pakistan's Babur cruise missile. These had been copied from the US Tomahawk missile after six of them crash-landed in Pakistan in 2001 during a US air strike in Afghanistan. They were not the Shaheen warheads thought to have been removed from Khushab.

Gunn heard the muffled noise of the confrontation by the side of the lorry, but other than placing his Glock beside him ready for instant use, he concentrated on hiding the IED which Simon Brewer had given him. He pulled some of the straw sacks out of the way and hid the device tight up against the two crates. He crawled back to the hole in the lorry's side curtain and gingerly peered out. The rest of the team were waiting like an athletic relay team preparing for the 'off!' from the starter's gun.

'Ready?' Gunn queried in a whisper.

'All ready, John,' was said in unison.

Gunn pulled back into the lorry, climbed over the sacks until he had a good view of the IED in the beam of his torch. He checked his watch which he'd zeroed with Simon's before leaving the CIA's weapon shop. Thirty seconds to go . . . . 10,9,8,7,6,5,4,3,2,1 . . . . shots and shouting erupted somewhere in the distance and the commotion gradually grew and came closer. Gunn reached out, lifted the protecting cover on the electronic timing device and made the connection. Immediately the IED came to life and the counter started its count down from 180 seconds. Gunn replaced all the sacks to hide the IED and then climbed down from the lorry.

'Time to go, lady and gentlemen,' and the group left the area beside the lorry and followed Emma and her cooking pot into the open area where most of the Taliban were now involved in the disturbance created by Simon and his recruits. The Taliban's immediate and utterly pointless reaction was to fire off their AK47s into the air which heightened the confusion and gave Emma and those following her perfect cover. Only a few more yards and they would be out of sight of the guards . . . . just a few more yards. The shouts grew louder and there was a general move of the gun-waving mob away from the bazaar area of the village.

Then came the shriek of fury which Gunn had been dreading. The shout was taken up by one after another of the mob closest to the lorry, now about one hundred yards behind Emma and her followers. Gunn glanced quickly at his watch . . . . it couldn't be more than 20 or 30 seconds to go. Gunn looked back again only to see the guards and other Taliban swarming into the back of the lorry like bees entering a hive.

Two things happened simultaneously . . . . what seemed like two of Zeus' thunderbolts roared overhead as the Hellfire missiles homed in on the lorry which, at the same instant, was enveloped in a vivid orange and red mushroom cloud as the IED exploded. The explosion was so powerful that everyone within a hundred yards of the lorry was thrown to the ground. Emma threw away her cooking pot and ran with the men into the street through the bazaar. People were running in all directions so no one took any notice of them. They found the Toyota where they had left it on Simon's advice. Emma, Doyle and the Ambassador got into the back and Javed joined Gunn in the front. Gingerly Gunn threaded his way through the crowd until they reached the outskirts of the village where the road did a switchback on itself and started the climb up the base of Tirich Mir to the Dorah Pass and Afghanistan.

'Anything following us,' Gunn asked as he peered through the smoke drifting across the road from the remains of the burning lorry and the shacks and huts closest to it.

'Not as far as I can see,' but they'll have two-way radios, so might have alerted the border which is almost entirely manned by border guards sympathetic to the Taliban cause,' Doyle replied after leaning out of the back window to get a better view.

'How far to the border check point?' Gunn asked.

'About 7 or 8 miles from here; they'll have heard the explosion so we must expect them to be ready for any vehicle approaching from the direction of the village,' Javed replied. He had the map-reading light on and was peering closely at the map. 'I'm going to suggest that we stop about two hundred yards short of the border. Doyle and I will take the AK47s and move to a position covering the border and the men manning it. We've still got those radios which we took from McCulloch and Crawford-Slade. We'll let you know when we're in position and then you drive to the border. Emma, do you have that other burka handy?'

'Yes, it's in my carrier bag.'

'Chuck I'm going to ask you to wear the other burka.'

'No problem,' and he took the burka from Emma who helped him put it on.

'Whatever happens, drive through the border and wait for Doyle and me about a hundred yards on the other side in Afghanistan. We can keep in contact with the radios. Anyone have any other suggestions?' Javed asked. No one offered any alternative plans. 'Right, we should be quite close to the border in about five minutes so let's get our weapons ready and check that the radios are still working.'

They were closer to the border than they thought and Gunn only just switched off the headlights in time for him to pull the SUV into a passing place tight up against the rock-face where the road had been blasted out of the mountain. Doyle and Javed got out of the car.

'Here, take these,' and Gunn handed his binoculars to Javed. They switched on the radios, did a radio check and then Doyle and Javed vanished into the darkness. The road from Garam Chasma to the border was a switchback all the way so from where they were parked there was an excellent view of the village, now about a thousand metres below them. Gunn was out of the car watching both the village and the road back to the last bend they had rounded before pulling in to the lay-by. Even as he watched, he saw the lights of two vehicles leave the village taking the same road as them up to the border. 'That had to be the pursuit group,' Gunn guessed, 'which has finally stopped its pointless occupation of firing ammunition into the air and has discovered that it has lost both the warheads and the Ambassador.' He was about to check the radio when it gave a bleep to alert him. He pressed the transmit switch. 'Gunn.'

'Javed, we should be in position in one minute. Any sign of pursuit?'

'Two vehicles have just left Garam Chasma.'

'OK, drive to the border post now.'

'Roger,' and Gunn climbed back into the SUV and drove out onto the road having placed his Glock in the glove compartment on his right. He put the headlights on full beam to make it as difficult as possible for the guards to identify the vehicle and its passengers until the very last moment.

As soon as the Toyota rounded the final bend before the border post, its arrival was greeted with shouts and a considerable amount of gesticulation.

'Just a warning guys; we have absolutely no way of bluffing our way through the border so it's a situation of shoot first and answer any questions later. Ready both of you?'

'Ready,' came from the Ambassador in his burka in the back and Emma in the front seat. The scene at the border stuck in Emma's memory for some considerable time. The whole area was illuminated by blindingly powerful floodlights which showed the border guards taking up fire positions.

'Get down!' Gunn shouted at his two passengers and as they obeyed the windscreen was shattered by a bullet which went through the vehicle and out of the tailgate window. Gunn pushed out the pulverised glass as a hail of bullets pinned down the border guards coming from a totally unexpected area overlooking the border. Gunn, Emma and the Ambassador had their windows down and as Gunn floored the accelerator, all three of them fired a volley of shots . . . . not hitting any target, but no one was going to raise their heads at what appeared to be overwhelming odds attacking the post. The Toyota raced through the border splintering the barrier pole which had been lowered across the road.

The suppressing fire from Doyle and Javed continued until the Toyota rounded the first bend of the descent from the Dorah Pass into Afghanistan. Gunn then pulled into the side of the road and switched on his satellite phone to transmit the code word RAT-TRAP. They were in a reasonably level area at the top of the pass before it began its switchback descent.

Doyle and Javed appeared over the top of a rock outcrop and slithered down a shale bank onto the road.

'We'll hold off any attempt to follow while we wait for the chopper,' Javed gasped, not used to the vigorous speed at which Doyle had led him over the rugged terrain to avoid the border post.

'Is there . . . .' but what ever Doyle was about to ask was drowned by the swishing thud, thud, thud of the silenced rotor of the Pave Hawk helicopter as it hovered above the Toyota. Gunn grabbed his torch and scrambled over the rocky ground to the flattest piece he could find and waved in the helicopter. Emma and the Ambassador picked up all the kit they could from the Toyota and followed Gunn. Javed was only a short distance behind them, while Doyle was down on the road with a view back to the border post.

Two Marines jumped from the helicopter and helped the Ambassador and then Emma into the Hawk. Javed followed while Gunn went back to where Doyle was crouched behind some rocks at the side of the road.

'I won't be more than a couple of seconds! John; I don't want those hooligans shooting at the chopper.' As he spoke, the other lorry belonging to Mubashar ali Munda drove through the border post. Doyle took very careful aim with his AK47 and then emptied the entire magazine into the windscreen. The lorry veered off the road, bounced and bumped over the rough ground with men jumping out of the back as it went until it ran out of mountain and pitched over the edge into the void below.

The two men scrambled back to the helicopter where they were helped aboard and sank down on the metal floor as the Hawk lifted off for its flight back to the joint US/UK military headquarters at Camp Bastion in Afghanistan's Helmand Provence via a mid course refuel.

CHAPTER 22

'Come in, John,' Sir Miles Thompson greeted Gunn, getting up from behind his desk, 'that was a very satisfactory conclusion to the operation in Pakistan. Coffee please Angela,' the Director of BID requested as his PA stuck her head round the door. 'You can ignore the usual nonsense published by the more extreme broadsheets and tabloids which accuse the US of an unprovoked attack on a Pakistani village killing dozens of women and children. But they all failed to mention that it removed the self-styled leader of the Pakistan Taliban, Mubashar ali Munda, who had hijacked two nuclear warheads and kidnapped the US Ambassador to Islamabad. I have had a message of sincere thanks—unofficial of course—from Pakistan's President, His Excellency Azil Zadari and the PM, Wasem Halabi. The US Secretary of State phoned our PM to express the President's and his gratitude for the successful outcome of the rescue.'

'What about the UK end of what I believe was called Operation Breakback,' Gunn queried sipping the scalding hot cup of espresso coffee and then continued after leaving the coffee to cool, 'after the arrest of Martin Whistler, they must have discovered who was master-minding the import of huge quantities of heroin from Afghanistan?'

'Your first suspicions were half right, but if I remember rightly you hadn't decided whether it was the Marquess of Purbeck or the gunsmith, Nathanial Breakspear. What put you on to those two?' the Director asked.

'Richard Jardine because of his skill with guns and the vast Cranborne debt to HMRC. Breakspear, because I just couldn't believe that wally of assistant gamekeeper, Alec Moore, was skilled enough to sabotage those shotguns in such a short time and in near darkness. But Breakspear did his utmost to throw us all off the scent, even using those evil smelling French cigarettes which Alec Moore smoked and providing him with that highly poisonous toxin to silence Tullet and me. Presumably it was Breakspear who drove Richard Jardine's Range Rover up to Universal Switchgear having been told by Preston that I was going there for a couple of days.'

'I expect so, fortunately, we were on to Preston by then, but had no idea how deeply he and his PA were involved. The ISI interrogation of Whistler confirmed all our suspicions and gave Detective Chief Inspector Nesbit the pleasure of wrapping up the case by arresting Breakspear.'

'So at least fifty percent of my assignment was to expose Preston and his PA. What a tragedy that it took the lives of three BID staff to achieve that, and Cala Williamson who I thought was the 'Mata Hari' of the shoot at Granvil Hall, turned out to be squeaky clean,' Gunn admitted. 'Presumably, the conversation that Tullet overheard was her trying to persuade her father to have nothing to do with the nuclear warheads. I suppose she brought that character Malouf to the shoot to prevent her father from doing something he might bitterly regret.'

'So it would seem, John.'

'Sadly, Tullet probably only picked up the bit about 'warheads and Taliban'. Shows how dangerous eaves-dropping can be.'

'Would it surprise you to learn that a certain Emma Pankhurst has submitted an application to join BID?'

'Not at all, sir. I'd be happy to act as a referee for her application.'

'Now why doesn't that surprise me? I believe we still have a mole in this building, but getting rid of that person will be your next assignment. In the meantime I suggest that you take that week of leave your missed.'

'Thank you, sir,' and Gunn left the Director's office.

OTHER BOOKS FEATURING JOHN GUNN

BY BRIAN NICHOLSON

GWEILO

The theft of a birthright has been the motive for murder since Jacob usurped it from his elder brother Esau. The loss of the birthright to the immense riches of Hong Kong leads to a plot by two men, one Chinese and the other a 'gweilo'—a descendant of the first settlers to arrive in Hong Kong. The catastrophic meltdown of the Chernobyl nuclear power station provides the solution—the destruction of Hong Kong rather than hand it back to the China. Fluent in both Cantonese and Mandarin Chinese, John Gunn is recruited for this assignment by the British Intelligence Directorate. But the countdown to this nuclear holocaust has already begun.

AL SAMAK

This is a rocket-paced thriller about a conspiracy by die-hard communists to sell nuclear warheads to Saddam Hussein. The conspirators are led by an ex-KGB psychopath whose bloodthirsty brutality even sickened the KGB and the Soviet leadership. Their choice of arms dealer is Hassan Hussein whose Kurdish village has been destroyed by Saddam's chemical gas attack. Horribly disfigured by the gas attack, Hassan has his own plans for the nuclear warheads. This is John Gunn's second assignment with the British Intelligence Directorate. It's a story of intrigue, treachery, revenge and unbelievable violence during the summer of 2002 when the USA, UK and IAEA were searching for the 'smoking gun' to justify the invasion of Iraq.

ASHANTI GOLD

The priceless ingots of Ashanti Gold are secured in the vaults of the Bank of Ghana. Gold will buy weapons and weapons are needed by the West African exiles, ruthless arms dealers, corrupt diplomats and politicians on both sides of the Atlantic conspiring to overthrow the governments of all West African countries. This is John Gunn's third assignment with the British Intelligence Directorate which has sent him to Ghana to investigate the disappearance of an SIS agent from the British High Commission.

FIRE DRAGON

Colliding tectonic plates, erupting volcanoes, earthquakes and tsunamis make Indonesia the most volatile geological archipelago in the World. This explosively unstable geology is matched by the volatile conspiracy of Romano Rusman who is determined to return Indonesia to a communist dictatorship. He has stumbled on the vast treasure hidden by Admiral Yamamoto at the end of World War 2 and uses this limitless source of funding to conspire with North Korea to place its nuclear weapons in space orbit out of the reach of the IAEA inspections and US spy satellites. A fatal error occurs while the nuclear warheads are being shipped from North Korea to Indonesia, which results in John Gunn's fourth assignment with the British Intelligence Directorate and his confrontation with man-eating komodo dragons in the 'ring of fire'.

CALYPSO

How can five yachts disappear without trace on a Caribbean cruise? What has happened to the British Warship sent to investigate? Where are Iraq's chemical weapons? Why is London lobbying for the release of a Camp Delta prisoner and why has a WW2 Dakota been shipped to the UK from the Mojave Desert? John Gunn is pitched into a desperate race against time on this assignment for the British Intelligence Directorate, as the answers to these questions reveal a conspiracy for a catastrophic terrorist atrocity in London.

SHARK

What is the secret that lies buried in the sand of the Iraqi Desert and why has this led to the murder of a British Intelligence agent? What was the name the gunman tried to utter before he died? Who is blackmailing senior members of the Cabinet Office and Intelligence Services? Who was the eighth man and who is the mole crippling the British Intelligence Directorate? Desperate urgency is needed to answer these questions because the next agent to be murdered is John Gunn.

TRAITOR

The spectre of a traitor who betrayed fellow soldiers in a Japanese POW camp in Hong Kong has risen from the grave to haunt the British Intelligence Directorate. A deliberate hit-and-run murder in London of the son of an ex-POW is followed by the murder of an agent during a break-in at Gunn's London house to search for war crime papers and diaries relating to the betrayal in 1941. Twice Gunn escapes the 21st Century Samurai warriors from a proscribed Japanese Mafia cult thought to have been responsible for the Sarin gas attack on the Tokyo subway.

Every effort is made by both the Director of the British Intelligence Directorate and the Japanese Mafia to prevent him taking over the investigation. This turns Gunn into a fugitive from the British police and the Counter-Espionage Department of BID as his search inevitably leads him back to Japan.

ASSASSIN

Decapitated and mutilated cadavers are discovered in the USA, UK, Sweden and Belgium. The MO in each incident is identical. The victims are linked by a package tour to Russia. Three members of that tour are still alive . . . . but for how long? And what is the connection to KAL Flight 007 shot down by the Soviet Union in 1983?

The British Intelligence Directorate and the CIA are pitched into a race to save the survivors of the package tour and expose double agents in their own intelligence organisations.

This latest assignment for BID agents John Gunn and Tanya Kazakova and the CIA's Doyle Barnes takes them into the bleak forest wilderness of the Russian Taiga.

SHOOT

For a 'dare', two small boys climb over the wall into the the Duke of Cranborne's estate in Hampshire. Both boys are armed with airguns, but what starts as a dare ends in blind terror for one of them as he stumbles in the dark across the body of a man whose head has been blown off. The man is a BID agent and his death jeopardises the security of a shoot organised for the Prime Ministers of several countries before the G20 Summit in London. John Gunn replaces the murdered agent and has to unravel a conspiracy involving nuclear weapons and drugs. From the lush grounds of the Cranborne estate in Hampshire to the bleak and inhospitable mountains of Pakistan's North West Frontier Provence, Gunn's assignment moves at breakneck speed to prevent the nuclear weapons reaching the Taliban and the heroin reaching the streets of the UK.

THE AUTHOR

Excitement started at an early age for the author; returning from India with his family in June 1945, aged 3, the ship in which the family was embarked was chased by a Japanese submarine which fortunately had run out of torpedoes. Brian Nicholson had an equally exciting career in the army for 35 years of which the last 10 were spent working with the officers of the Secret Intelligence Service in various overseas appointments in Hong Kong, Ghana and Indonesia.

He was made an OBE in 1985 and received a Commendation from the Commander British Forces Hong Kong in 1987 for his success in the negotiations with the Chinese Government on the handover of Hong Kong. At the request of the Royal Navy Funeral Department, while he was Defence Attaché in Jakarta, he solved the mystery of what happened to Sub-Lieutenant Gregor Riggs. Riggs was the last of the 23 Commandoes on the ill-fated Australian Commando raid, Operation Rimau, on Japanese shipping in Singapore Harbour in World War 2. The author discovered the remains of the young officer on a remote island in the Indonesian Archipelago and returned them to the family for burial with full military honours at the Changi Military Cemetery in Singapore.

In 1990, as Military Advisor to Jerry Rawlings, Ghana's President, he was directed to plan the successful West African military intervention in Liberia after the horrific videoed torture and assassination of the country's despotic dictator, Master Sergeant Samuel Doe. These are but a few of the exciting experiences in a colourful career which formed the backdrop to the nine books which he has written. He is currently researching his ninth book. Brian Nicholson is married with two adult daughters and lives in Richmond where his time is taken up with writing, golf, shooting and sailing.

THE AUTHOR

BRIAN NICHOLSON

Lightning Source UK Ltd.
Milton Keynes UK
UKOW04f2252250717

306058UK00001B/28/P